HIS REAL NAME IS AARON

outskirts
press™

CHAPTER 1

Most people avoided Florida Street if they could. It was a small one-way downtown with parking on each side. An open spot was always hard to find and almost impossible because of the businesses that lined it. Traffic didn't move quickly. There was the Dooner Sausage company that made and sold their own sausage. It had a small parking lot for customers, but when it filled up, they scrambled to get spots on the street. The sausage was just that good and the aroma filled the nearby downtown area. Dooner even had its own breakfast café.

Florida Street was only a block long and the sausage company took up one whole side. A bookstore, coffee shop, and a department store corporate office called Ward's, took up the other side. Florida Street ended at the First Star Bank with its customers leaving the drive-thru tellers, only being able to turn left or right onto Crane Ave. Traffic on Florida could only turn left onto Crane. It was an access to the freeway out of busy downtown, but only the right lane led to it. The far-left lane led back to the downtown streets, which Dooner Sausage customers mainly took to look for parking.

Deena worked on Florida Street at Ward's, but parked in a structure on a different street around the corner. She left work early to meet her grandmother for a doctor's appointment. She always rounded the corner on the small crammed street to get to the freeway. She had a habit of leaving her cell phone in her work desk and pulled over at the Dooner Sausage loading zone to quickly check her purse for it.

"Thank God I didn't forget," she said to herself.

She didn't want to let her grandmother down. She put the car in gear and signaled to pull away when it stalled. She turned it off, started it again and went nowhere.

"Dammit! This is not happening to me!" she screamed.

Her insides instantly got hot, and she didn't know what to do except turn it off and start it again. She certainly wasn't going to get out and check under the hood. She wouldn't know what to look for, let alone how to fix it. She jumped suddenly at someone knocking on her passenger side window. The Dooner Sausage delivery driver was leaning down looking into her car. She stared back without saying anything as if to ask, 'What?'

"You can't park here. I can't get through," the driver said loudly while pointing back at his truck.

Not realizing she pulled over and blocked a loading zone, she silently panicked.

"I can't move! My car shut off!" she yelled.

A man walked up to the delivery driver. It was Shawn.

He worked for Dooner Sausage as a stock person and unloaded the trucks. He had walked through the building down to the loading dock to meet the afternoon driver with the last delivery. He didn't see him and knew he was probably running behind, as had been the case lately.

"I wish they would do something about him," he mumbled, pushing the words from his mouth with his teeth clenched together.

He had to stay past his shift each time a driver was late. He threw his hands in the air and slammed them to his sides in frustration. He looked outside and saw him stopped in the street with traffic backed up behind him.

Shawn jumped down from the dock and made his way over to him. He saw Deena's car in front of the loading zone.

"What's going on?" He asked the driver.

"Her car stopped and I can't get in here," he said.

Deena turned the key in the ignition back and forth desperately with a nervous look. This was going to keep her from meeting her grandmother. She knew going back to get her phone would've made her late, but this was making her miss the appointment altogether.

"Don't do that," Shawn said, standing at her driver's side window. "You're gonna mess up something. You're battery's probably dead."

Deena didn't see that he walked to her side of the car. Her window was half-way down. She sighed and stared straight ahead.

"Can we just push you up a little bit so he can get his truck in here?" Shawn asked as if he was in a hurry.

"Yeah. Thank you so much and I'm so sorry about this," she said.

"No problem. Can you put it in neutral?" Shawn was serious and still in a hurry.

The driver walked back to the truck and drove out of the other side of the parking lot to come around again and make his second attempt to back the truck up to the dock.

Deena put the car in neutral still thinking about her grandmother. She would be telling her doctor to wait for Deena before discussing any issues about her health. Deena kept up with her medications and appointments. She especially checked almost daily to make sure her grandmother followed her doctor's instructions.

"I'm just gonna call and let them know I can't make it," she said to herself.

She would have the doctor write down any new concerns and give it to her grandmother and follow up later if need be.

"That's it. I'll just do that," she said, relieved at the idea.

It would be a first, but it would work.

The car slowly moved forward and Shawn was behind it. He only pushed her about two car lengths ahead and stopped. She was still in the no-parking zone, but out of the way.

"Okay, you all good?" He asked.

"Yes. Thank you so much. And I apologize for being in the way. I didn't realize where I pulled over."

"No problem. You have a good day," Shawn said, rushing back over to the loading dock.

He grabbed box after box off the truck, unloading it as fast as he could. He hated working past his normal hours. He signed the driver's delivery sheet and handed it back without looking at him. He knew the driver was late, but felt it was no point in confronting him once again about it, especially since he would just blame it on a car blocking the entrance. He walked away from the truck, put the delivery away, and quickly punched his end time on the clock.

He had not been interested in college after high school, but now he longed for the corporate salaries of the business men he saw walking by day-to-day. He was thirty-three years old and had mostly worked factory jobs, doing loading and forklift driving. He stood most of the day as usual, and couldn't wait to get home and relax. It had been a long day.

He left the building from the front entrance and saw Deena still there in her car, parked where he pushed her earlier. It had been at least forty-five minutes and he was surprised to see her, figuring someone would have met her there by then.

"That's a first," he thought.

Seeing a woman whose car stopped working, and she wasn't on a cell phone at least talking with a girlfriend while she waited for help. Even though he wanted to get as far away from Dooner Sausage as he could, he walked over to her car.

Deena saw him walking toward her with his eyes on hers. She knew he was coming to see why she was still there. He stopped at her front bumper and she stepped out of the car and walked over to him.

"I'm just waiting on a tow truck that should be on the way," she said, putting her hand out to shake his. "Thanks again for helping me."

"Oh no problem. I came over because I was leaving and saw you still here. You need a ride home?"

"No," Deena giggled. She was embarrassed to say. "The two people that could've picked me up won't be able to get here for at least two hours, so." She paused, even more embarrassed. "I'm gonna get a ride from the tow truck driver."

She was disgusted at the idea of having to ride with a rough looking, dirty, beard-to-his-chest, ashtray smelling, tow truck driver. She pictured all tow truck drivers that way.

"Okay that look you gave says you *really* don't wanna do that," Shawn said laughing. "I can give you a ride home. I know I'm technically a stranger, but you let a stranger push your car out of the way earlier," he joked.

Deena laughed and then smiled at him, unsure of whether to accept his ride or ride in a filthy tow truck with a driver to match.

"My name is Shawn Buchanan. My date of birth is 11-09-73. You want my address and social security number too?" Shawn blurted it out quickly, interrupting Deena's thoughts.

She giggled, still not giving an answer.

"You know where I work," Shawn said, pointing to the building. "And on top of that this damn place has cameras all around it! If I wanted to kidnap you, I'm asking to go to jail!"

He hadn't really focused on her earlier. His frustration with the late delivery driver distracted him from really noticing her. Now he saw every bit of her.

Her green sun dress fell over her curved hips just right and her silver jewelry complimented her brown skin. She was natural. Only eyeliner and lipstick made up her face and sunglasses held her flowing hair down and completed her simple accessories. She was not overdone. She was just right.

"Okay," she said, "but I don't wanna hold you up. The tow truck still isn't here."

She thought he was charming and funny, not to mention good looking. She hadn't noticed him earlier, either. All she could think about then was her grandmother and why her car suddenly stopped.

The tow truck arrived, slowing down as it got near them and Deena waved her hand to the driver, getting his attention.

He was large with a full beard and long, greasy ponytail that hung down to the middle of his back. He wore a dirty baseball cap turned backwards and his t-shirt was torn at the bottom and overstretched on his huge belly.

Deena walked to the truck and gave him her information. She paid him and walked back over to Shawn. They waited until the car was hooked up to the truck before leaving.

They both looked at each other and shared a giggle.

"Why do they all look like that?" she said, laughing about the tow truck driver. "Do they get hired based on how dirty and scruffy they are?"

"See, aren't you glad you accepted my ride? He was gonna eat you," Shawn joked.

He drove her home and they exchanged phone numbers.

———◉———

Their first date was at a coffee shop on the east side of town and afterward, they walked through Gardens Park. Deena didn't drink tea or coffee. She was satisfied with a glass of water and a biscotti.

She loved Gardens Park though. It was made up of all different plants and flowers with walkways throughout. She didn't dare walk through there alone because it was certainly lovers' territory. The one and only time she had been was with a guy who made it apparent that other things like the never-ending phone calls on his cell were more important. It didn't take her long to figure out what he was about. Working at a car wash but driving a souped-up limited-edition

Mercedes Benz truck didn't quite add up. It paired well with his quick one or two-word responses to the phone calls he got when they hooked up.

She had no tolerance for drug dealers and knew it was dangerous to be around them. She pictured herself in his passenger seat being shot by someone at a stop light with him being the intended target. Leaving him was a no-brainer.

She was happy to be there with Shawn and she could tell he was happy too. He listened. He laughed at her jokes and was interested in what she had to say. They talked all night and told each other their life stories.

Deena couldn't be happier her car broke down. She probably wouldn't have met him otherwise. It had been three days since then, and she was tickled at the thought.

CHAPTER 2

"I've been trying to get a hold of you for the longest. What's up with you? You usually call me back," Angie said desperately talking to Deena's voicemail.

She had the weekend to herself. Her six-year old daughter Tia was with her dad, and Bruce her every-now-and-then companion was out of town. So, he said.

Bruce was not worthy of being called a boyfriend. He didn't do boyfriend things, but she put up with it. After all, she had not found someone right for her yet, and accepted Bruce's company and sex in the meantime.

It was going on day three that she hadn't heard from Deena. She wanted to go out for drinks at Push. It was the new talked about spot downtown. She had a chance to finally go, but knew Deena probably wouldn't go for it if she did get a hold of her.

Deena didn't drink much. At least not like someone who went out to clubs. She was not the club type and hated crowds. Angie liked to get out sometimes, but really only did it with her cousin Kayla. She was sick with food poisoning that weekend, so Deena was Angie's only hope.

She and Deena had been best friends since high school.

Angie met Brian and got pregnant with Tia not long after. He was a good father to Tia and spent a lot of time with her. He and Angie stopped getting along and grew apart when Tia was around two years old, but they stayed good friends.

"I'll be damned if I waste my whole weekend doing nothing," Angie said.

The phone rang and she picked it up on the first ring.

"Hello."

"I know you're gonna kill me for not calling you back," Deena said.

"Girl! You had me kinda worried for a minute. I almost drove over and banged on your door."

Deena laughed.

"My car broke down the other day remember? I called you that night but you couldn't talk long because that sometimey ass Bruce was over there. I get put on the back burner when he comes around."

"No. You know it's not like that," Angie laughed.

"That's alright. Because you're about to get put on the back burner too. I met somebody and my nose is open already."

"What?! Who is he?" Angie asked, happily surprised.

"I met him when my car broke down. His name is Shawn."

Deena told Angie how they met and how since

then she's run down her cell phone battery several times in the last few days talking to him. Shawn was definitely a breath of fresh air and her not getting enough sleep at night was proof of that.

"Well good for you! Uh oh. I'm in trouble then. Guess I won't hear from you much anymore," Angie laughed.

"Oh please. I'm not like you. I don't forget about my friends. But I *will* give you a taste of your own medicine though. And it'll be worth it. Unlike that loser Bruce. He's only good for one thing."

Deena always told Angie a piece of her mind when it came to the men she chose to deal with. Angie took it well and laughed it off, but Deena was serious. She knew Angie could do better.

They were night and day when it came to picking men. Deena didn't see what was sexy about a guy who always claimed to be looking for a job and flopping on his mother's couch. And it seemed Angie didn't mind that at all. She always justified it with, 'He's trying to find a job' or 'he works on houses sometimes with his uncle.' Deena thought, the worse off they were, the better the sex must've been.

She didn't know where Angie went wrong after Tia's dad. He still worked in the grocery store where he was once just a cart pusher and was now the manager. He bought a house and was engaged to be married soon. She never found anyone else with his level of determination and drive, and she didn't seem to be looking for it, either.

"What are you doing tonight? Let's do something," Angie said excitedly. "Unless you're doing somethin' with your new man."

"No, we went out last night and tonight he said he was gonna take out a friend of his who flew in town today. So, what's up?"

"Well, I *really really* wanna go to Push."

Angie quickly held the phone way out from her so she wouldn't have to hear Deena's "hell nos" loud in her ear.

"Ok, I'll do it. What time?" Deena simply said.

"Oh my God! Say that again?!"

Angie couldn't believe it.

"I said I'll go."

"Then you *must* be love struck!" Angie shouted. "What did this man do to my friend?!"

"There is nothing wrong with me. Will you stop all that?"

"Girl, you never wanna go out. You're a go-to-a-restaurant and every-now-and-then have a drink chick. Not a go-to-the-club, shake-your-ass, get-your-drink-on chick. I just can't believe it. But before you change your mind, I'll be ready around nine."

"Don't get too happy. I'm not staying after twelve," Deena said.

"That's fine. I'll take what I can get Cinderella. I know your clock strikes at midnight."

Deena talked to Shawn every day at least twice. They still spent long hours on the phone at night and it became the norm for the next few weeks.

She got a call one Sunday night from her cousin Toni.

Her wedding was the following Saturday and she asked Deena to be a "last minute" bridesmaid because of some typical wedding drama between her and a friend. Toni had tried to tell her the reason one of her friend's dropped out of the wedding, but Deena didn't want to hear her dramatized, over-the-top explanation. Being her last resort, she obliged her and told her she would be in the wedding. It didn't hurt that her dress and shoes were already paid for. What did hurt was that she had to scramble in the new few days after work to get prepared.

She thought about Shawn and the fact that she wouldn't be able to see him at all that week. They had planned to go see a movie, but she had to cancel. With all her running around, she barely got to talk to him except for later at night. She got to know him even more from their talks on the phone, and she craved to see him again. The only time she could see him was well after midnight, and that wasn't her style. She wasn't into giving the wrong impression, especially if she really liked the person.

She had told him about the wedding and the rest of her week being tied up by it. It was flattering to hear genuine disappointment in his voice and she smiled to herself thinking about it.

Was he the one?

She had asked herself this about a guy too many times. But something about Shawn was different. He called her two or three times a day just to say hi and that he was thinking about her. Even though she was over the moon, she didn't let on too much and decided to see how far he would go to show his infatuation.

Her cousin told her she was about the same size as her friend who dropped out of the wedding so she would probably not have to get the bridesmaid dress altered.

She was right.

Deena drove to pick up the dress from a seamstress and besides it being hunter green with an over-sized bow in the back, it fit perfect.

She walked back to her car in disgust.

"Why the hell would she put us in hunter green in July?!" She said to herself out loud. "Christmas is months away and this is a damn Christmas color. I feel like it should be snowing outside."

She couldn't get back to the car fast enough to call Angie.

"Hello."

"Hunter green?! Who the hell picks hunter green for a wedding color in the middle of summer?!"

"Are you serious? Your cousin is somethin' special," Angie said laughing. "Then why not get married in December?"

"That's what I'm saying! This girl has lost her

mind. And the dress is down-right ugly. Wait until you see this humongous bow in the back. But it's my fault for not asking questions first. I just told her I would do it, but this is so not my style. I wonder did any of her friends talk to her about that?"

"Well, you know if they did, she obviously didn't listen. And what the bride wants is how it goes. But that's on her. She's the one that's gonna have a photo album with wedding colors that don't match the season," Angie said laughing.

"I don't wanna see what the shoes look like. As a matter of fact, I'm gonna tell her I can't pick 'em up, and make her go get 'em instead. Just for this ugly dress I gotta wear," Deena said. "I was on my way there next, but I'm about to call her and make her do it. I'll call you back."

She hung up with Angie and called Toni. She looked in her backseat at the dress and rolled her eyes hard, especially at the bow.

"Hello," Toni answered.

"Toni?"

"Yeah, it's me."

"This is Deena. I just picked up the dress, but I don't have time to get the shoes," she said, sounding like she was busy with something.

"Oh, okay. I'll either get 'em or try to have somebody else do it. Don't worry about it. I just appreciate you doing this for me on short notice. Everything is coming together and I'm happy that's the only problem I really had so far. I'll get the shoes and have 'em for you at the rehearsal. Thank you so much," she said.

Deena decided not to mention the look of the dress and felt it would upset Toni while she seemed so happy with everything. Maybe nobody else had said anything. It sure seemed that way with how giddy Toni was. Deena wondered what color the men were wearing. White tuxedos with green ties came into her head. She rolled her eyes.

"Okay, I'll see you at the rehearsal."

She hung up still picturing the wedding party at the church and in the photo album.

CHAPTER 3

A Blue Monday picture hung on the wall across from Deena's bed. She bought it because she looked like the woman in it almost every morning, let alone Mondays. The loud, annoying beep from her alarm clock at six o'clock is what planted her feet on the floor each morning, but that was all it did. She sat there on the bed slumped over staring at the floor. It was her snooze time. It didn't matter how many times she had done it, she hated to get up early. She made it a point to sleep late on weekends. At least that way, she didn't look like Blue Monday *every* day.

At 6:10, the alarm blared, and she raised her head to see if it was that time on the clock. Ten minutes was long enough to snooze. She gave herself just enough time to get ready. Her eyes hurt from being on the phone with Shawn until well after midnight. It didn't feel good not getting much sleep, but it was worth it. She knew his morning had to be the same because they both started work at 7:30. She never asked if his mornings were rough since they had been talking late every night, but she figured as much. She didn't know anyone who woke up cheerful, charged and ready for the day on only four or five hours of sleep.

She sure wasn't.

She looked up at Blue Monday and walked into the bathroom. She pressed a warm wet towel to her face and thought she heard a faint tapping noise somewhere. She stopped to concentrate on it, but didn't hear it again. She turned the water off and pulled her night scarf from her head. She heard light tapping again coming from her living room.

Someone was knocking on her door. Who was there and why at 6:15? That never happened. She was quiet and walked to the door.

It was Shawn.

Her heart beat quick. She was nervous.

Why had he come?

They talked until around one o'clock that morning and it was a work day. He knew where she lived but had never been inside. It had to be an emergency. But what?

All of this went through her head in seconds. She looked through the peep hole again before opening the door. She was glad she showered before bed. Her hair was a mess pressed down to her head, but it was no time to get it together. She had to open the door.

"Hi," he said, trying to make sure he spoke quietly.

"Hi."

"I know what time it is and I know you have to be at work. I have to be at work. I just need your help with somethin."

"What's that?"

Deena thought it had to be serious for him to show up at her place that early and unannounced.

"I got this certain woman on my mind and no matter what I do, I can't get her off. I was minding my own business one day and she just kinda fell into my life. I helped her with her car and offered her a ride home."

Deena's eyes widened as she listened.

Shawn continued.

"Now I have to call her at least two times a day to hear her voice. I gotta talk to her every night before I go to sleep. It's just something about her I can't shake. She told me she'd be busy all this week. A wedding or something? And I couldn't wait that long. I had to see her. So, can you help me?"

He was fixated on her.

Her eyes got even wider. She stepped back away from the door, holding it open. Her eyes gave her away and told him she felt the same way. Without another word, he pushed his body against hers and rushed his tongue into her mouth. She received him just the same, bracing herself to the blow of his solid chest on her and tilting her head back just in time to taste a long-awaited kiss. He held her and walked her backward. Her back pressed against the living room wall. Neither of them opened their eyes. Their tongues stayed locked. His hands moved down her sides and he slowed them at her butt, gently lifting it and squeezing while he pressed his upper body against her even harder. He didn't feel panties under her paper-thin sleep shirt and his insides wanted to burst. She never wore panties to bed. He raised one of her legs and she wrapped it around him. He was rock solid and could feel the front of his jeans against her. Her juices exploded on him every time he pushed against her. He kept one of her thighs up around his waist while he loosened his belt. His pants dropped and he entered her. The kiss was over and she held onto him squeezing while he moved up and down inside her.

They craved each other for a while and this was the one and only thing left to wonder about. There was no need to wonder anymore. It was good to both of them. Deena was won over by how he said he felt about her. The sex was even better than she expected.

———◉———

The wedding day finally came and it was on to the reception. Deena was not in the mood for dancing. She never liked going to weddings without a date or even better, a potential candidate on her arm. Like other women, she wanted it to be *her* day at the altar. She felt like Shawn was a candidate already, but he couldn't be there with her. She wouldn't see him until the next night.

She thought of him every second and imagined the two of them dancing with everyone else. She wore a simple, strapless off-white gown. Something about the pure white and virgin thing didn't sit right with her. Shawn was everything in his traditional black tux that held a silver handkerchief in the pocket to match her shoes. They danced with their noses touching. They giggled about having pulled everything off with no wedding drama. Her dress swayed back and forth while he held her close into him as they moved with the music. It blared loud throughout the room and gave them a chance to plan their escape later without anyone hearing them. Toward the end of the night, they'd slip off from their guests and head to their private room.

"Deena get up and dance girl!"

Toni had walked over to her and snapped her out of her day dream. It had been Toni dancing with her groom that Deena was watching when she drifted off, replacing them with her and Shawn.

"No, I'm tired. I don't really feel like dancing. Besides, my feet are killing me from earlier having to take all those pictures," Deena said to her in a joking but irritated way.

"Well, you gotta do it big. That's my motto," Toni said as she sashayed to the music in front of Deena.

"Oh. Is that what it is? Okay."

Deena smiled and tried to get the *I'd rather be somewhere else* look off her face. Toni pulled her arm trying to get her up from the chair. She was saved by her cell phone suddenly ringing. Toni let her arm go and she grabbed for it seeing that it was Shawn.

"Hey, you havin' a good time?" He asked.

"No. I'm glad you called. I've been thinking about you all day."

Deena had to almost scream into the phone. The music was so loud. Shawn said something and she couldn't hear a word. She pressed a finger in one ear and the phone hard against the other. She still couldn't quite hear him. She walked out of the reception room to hear better.

"I said come outside to the far end of the parking lot," he said.

"Are you here?!"

Deena was suddenly happy and nervous at the same time.

"Yes. Can I just get a quick kiss from you? I miss you."

Deena grabbed the bottom of her dress and pulled it up to run through the front doors of the venue out to the parking lot. She still held the phone to her ear with one hand.

"Are you there?" Shawn asked.

"I'm coming right now," she said sounding out of breath.

She found his car at the end of the lot and he got out and stood by it just before she made it to him. She jumped on him and flung her feet back, squeezing him tight. He had lifted her off the ground and carefully put her back down. They stood there and kissed. She pulled back from him and he still held her by the waist.

"I'm so happy to see you," she said. "But I'm so embarrassed you had to see me in this ugly dress."

She stepped back from him showing it.

"You wear the dress. It doesn't wear you."

Shawn stared straight at her.

"You look sexy in anything to me.

He pulled her toward him and kissed her again.

"My feet are killing me."

Deena frowned a little with a pained look on her face. She shifted her feet around in her shoes trying to stand still.

"Sit in the car for a minute," he said.

Shawn went around and opened the passenger door for her.

"How much time you got before they send the wedding police after you?"

They both laughed.

"Everybody's dancing and drinking. They probably didn't notice I was gone, but that damn Toni will after a while."

Deena sat in the car and Shawn closed the door. He ran around to his side and sat down.

"Well, I'll make it quick. Gimme your foot."

He held his hand out for Deena to put one of her feet out to him.

"What?"

"I said gimme one of your feet. You said they hurt."

Deena shifted herself on the seat and pressed her back against the door. The long bulky dress crunched when she moved around. She took off her left shoe and lifted her foot over the middle console. Shawn placed it on his lap and massaged it. They talked and Deena told him all about the wedding and how much standing they did for pictures. She closed her eyes most of the time because his hands felt good. She crossed one leg over the other so he could do her right foot.

He gave both her feet resuscitation to move about the rest of the night.

"Go get you a dance or two in," he said and giggled. "I'll let you get back in there, even though I wanna keep you with me."

"Now that I saw you, I just might do that," Deena laughed. "And I might just get myself a drink or two as well."

She thanked him for the foot massage and they kissed a long kiss again. She got out of the car and walked back inside. He watched her and then drove away.

CHAPTER 4

I f Angie's upstairs neighbors were home, they would've been annoyed by her loud TV that had been playing most of the morning. She almost slept the morning away and Tia watched cartoons after she got herself some cereal. Angie was in a deep sleep and hadn't heard how loud Tia had the TV with her favorite cartoon channel. She finally woke up and saw that it was eleven o'clock. She hadn't set her alarm and jumped up remembering she had to be at the downtown Roche Salon by noon. It was a six-week training for makeup artists and the first thirty applicants got half off the class.

Makeup was her thing, and hopefully after the training, she could get a job doing what she loved and kiss unemployment goodbye. This opportunity was good for her. She had worked as a receptionist for a trucking company, but was laid off when the business went under. She knew makeup inside and out and did it well.

The TV being so loud annoyed her.

"Tia turn that TV down and start getting ready! I gotta be somewhere by twelve o'clock and I overslept," Angie yelled.

Tia still faced the TV and watched the cartoon characters on the screen. They were getting ready for a showdown and was about to transform into their save-the-day characters to help the town overcome a disastrous storm. She stared and couldn't take her eyes off the TV until the mission was accomplished. She had seen the episode more than she could count, but it was her favorite. Angie had yelled more than once for her to start getting ready and turn the TV off. Tia only turned it down, but couldn't stop watching.

Angie walked into the living room.

"Tia, did you hear me? I said we gotta leave. Turn this off."

She held out a pair of shorts and a shirt to her. Tia took one last look at the sun character lighting up the town and turned the TV off. She went into her bedroom and changed her clothes. They headed to the door to leave.

"Where are we going?" She asked.

"Somewhere to hopefully get me a job."

Angie opened the door and Bruce was there with his hand raised about to knock. She jumped back.

"Whoa, you scared the hell out of me!" She yelled.

Bruce had never come to her apartment that early in the day. He always called first too.

"I was driving past and just stopped to see you. You leavin' out?"

"Yeah, I'm going downtown to sign up for this makeup class and I'm running behind."

"I can take you. I'm not doing anything."

Angie was shocked but she took him up on his offer. She and Tia ran to his car and got in. She knew she wouldn't have to look for parking at least. She was sure she had a spot in the class on the way there and she was happy inside. Bruce talked and she was happy to see him as always, but couldn't help wondering what his showing up was all about. It was out of the blue for him. The only time she saw him at that hour was when he was leaving her apartment from having spent the night.

"So, what'd you say this class is for?"

"It's a training for doing makeup. If I get in, I can get a job doing makeup at expo centers for makeup promotions or basically anywhere doing makeup."

"Oh, that's cool. You wanna go eat somewhere after you finish? Me, you, and Tia. It's on me."

Angie was taken aback.

"Go eat somewhere. It's on me," she thought to herself.

He'd never done that before. What was up with him? She certainly didn't want to pass up the offer considering Bruce hadn't spent a dime on her since they met. The two-for-two cheeseburgers he brought her from McDonald's one night after club hopping didn't count.

"Tia you wanna go out to eat when I get done? Bruce said he'll take us."

"Yeah, I wanna go," Tia said from the backseat.

"Okay. As if any kid is going to say no to going

out to eat," she laughed, looking over at Bruce. "That was a dumb question."

They pulled up near the Roche salon and Angie saw about twenty women walking inside in a single file line. She hoped she made it. She and Tia got out of the car and ran for the door. Angie counted the women in line in front of her. She was the twenty-eighth person and got the discount for the training. Her day had started off good.

Bruce waited for her and she thanked him for showing up and getting her there just in time. She was looking forward to spending time with him even though it was not clear what got into him all of a sudden. Maybe he finally saw she was the woman for him and he wanted to start a commitment. Or was it just some type of huge favor he wanted? If it was that, it couldn't be money. He knew she didn't have any. Angie didn't know what it could be and assumed he must've wanted a commitment.

Time would tell.

Without asking her preference of a restaurant, he pulled into the parking lot of Cooly's Soul Food. It happened to be owned by the family of his close friend. Angie didn't mind but knew he'd get a discount on their meal. It was all still a start for Bruce where she was concerned. They hadn't been out anywhere in public except for running into each other at a few clubs.

She had been craving soul food for a long time and Cooly's did have good food. They ate and Bruce took them home.

"What are you about to do?" He asked.

"Nothin. Why?"

"I was gonna come in and kick back with you for a while."

"Okay." Angie paused. "What's going on with you? It's only two o'clock and you actually wanna come in and stay for a while?"

"What? You act like I've never just chilled with you."

"You have, but not at two o'clock in the afternoon."

"Well, if you don't want me to, I can keep going," Bruce said, testing Angie's inability to say no to him.

She knew he was not as interested in their relationship, if it could be called that. She only hoped something would change his mind. Certainly, his wanting to stay at two o'clock in the afternoon was a start.

CHAPTER 5

September had come quick and summer was officially over. Bruce had moved in with Angie and settled into their relationship. So, it seemed. She was happy it had come to this and stopped questioning why he had finally done it in the first place. She couldn't help but think of what Deena had to say about it. That he was using her and probably had nowhere else to go. That whatever woman he was already living with had come to her senses and told him to beat it. That he was only in survival mode, which was actually twenty-four-seven. An opportunist. A man who knew how to sweet talk his way into a woman's heart as well as her house. Whatever name or description Deena could give him, she did. Angie ignored it and tried to put it out of her mind. It mattered that she had him with her at night. They laughed and cooked breakfast together in the mornings. They watched their favorite movies on rainy days. He even watched a few Lifetime ones with her. It was all good. She tried not to think about the fact that he still didn't have a job. Sometimes he'd help his uncle with some home improvement jobs, but he only made enough to pay his cell phone bill and treat her and Tia to a restaurant every now and then.

She had finished the cosmetician training and got a job at the mall kiosk selling a line of makeup advertised in an infomercial. It was more than unemployment paid, but money was still tight. Bruce was a third mouth to feed. She had to buy more food and toiletries. He ate much more than she and Tia and he slept with the TV on all night.

Tia's dad Brian started to give his opinion about the situation. He never said much about any of Angie's boyfriends and always told her it was her business who she chose to date. As long as Tia liked them and never complained to him about anything, he was okay. He had the father-daughter talk with her and was confident that it stuck.

His opinion didn't come from Tia's complaints, but from Angie's hand out more than usual. He didn't mind being a little more generous to her in addition to his child support payments and having Tia on weekends. But he had to be a lot more generous since Bruce moved in. Tia had told him Bruce didn't have a job.

Angie could only take his comments for so long. It was Deena in her ear all over again. She could take Deena's rips on Bruce. She couldn't and wouldn't take them from an ex, especially her child's father. It kept her from asking him for any more favors. She hated Bruce being compared to him. It was definitely a knock against her that she seemed so desperate for a man, she settled for anything that came her way. She didn't feel it was the case. She saw potential in Bruce and thought he just needed a woman that would push him to the next level. A lot of men met good women and just didn't realize it at first. It's all about sex for them in the beginning--and sometimes all the while. But every man eventually sees a woman's worth and gets his act together to be her man and *only* her man.

This went through Angie's mind. To her, Bruce realized she was the best woman for him. What could be another reason him moving in with her? She didn't feel there *was* one. All she had to do now was push him to that next level.

She felt sorry for him. He told her grew up in foster care and never knew his parents. It was all he would say once when she asked him about his mother. He said he didn't like talking about it. All she knew in the past two months about his family was the uncle he mentioned. If he never knew his parents and grew up in foster care, who was this uncle? Foster care does not mean adopted so she couldn't help but wonder.

It wasn't the time to try to investigate.

The bills were piling up and took priority over other stuff. Since asking Brian was no longer an option, Angie had no one else to get money from. Her mother wasn't even a last resort.

They stopped getting along when Angie got pregnant with Tia. Her mother was all about image. She never told anyone about any problems she had. Angie remembered one time when her mother had no money to buy groceries and had to rely on a food pantry so the two of them could eat. She put on a long wig, a hat, and dark sunglasses so she wouldn't be recognized in the line. She made Angie wear a hooded sweater with the hood pulled over her head the whole time, tied tightly under her chin, just in case any of her class-mates should happen to be in line with their parents. She did what she was told and stared at the ground and never looked up. They waited in line over an hour. They had to do it a few times and no one ever knew.

Her mother tried to keep friends who lived the "Jones'" lifestyle, while she only dreamt about it. She spent her money on expensive clothes and got her hair done every two weeks at the salon. They hardly had visitors at their small apartment because she told people they lived in a ritzy suburb condo, knowing full well they didn't. She worked as a receptionist for an insurance company, but went around saying she was an insurance underwriter. She was snooty and hardly associated with anyone she felt was "beneath" her. She made Angie tell lies about how they lived and what they could afford should anyone ask. So, of course it embarrassed her that Angie was pregnant so soon after high school. She never told her high-class friends she was going to be a grandmother. She had bragged to them of plans to get Angie into a model-ing agency. That was out the window. Angie wasn't the least bit interested anyway, but never thought she'd endure her mother cursing her and in so many words, hating her for getting pregnant. It had been years since they spoke and she had only seen Tia twice since she was born. Angie could never get over it. How could her mother be such a selfish bitch? Tia had only known her father's mother as *grandma.* Angie had to remind herself of what her mother was like and always felt like she had to come to her senses. She didn't know if she ever wanted Tia to know her after all.

The front door suddenly closed and her bitch of a mother left her thoughts.

Bruce came in with a catfish dinner in a foam to-go container. The smell made it through the door before he did. He didn't look at her. Something in his ears distracted him from everything else.

Those damn headphones. He had music playing. He pulled them backwards and off his head and took off his coat. The outside world had come back to him.

He finally noticed her.

"What's up baby?"

He sat down right away and dug in. Angie saw one platter come out of the bag. He didn't ask if she wanted some. Three people lived there and he boldly walked in with one fish platter and didn't even offer any. Where had he got the money for it?

Angie was pissed. She was in the middle of thinking about how to pay the bills and in he comes with one plate of food. There was no better time to have that conversation of pushing him to the next level. He needed to get a job.

CHAPTER 6

Even though Dooner Sausage was always the last place Shawn wanted to see, he looked forward to going to work because Deena was right across the street at Ward's. He couldn't leave the building for lunch, but she could. He managed to talk his supervisor into letting her join him for lunch every day in the employee break room. They had been seeing each other by then for almost six months. They took turns packing lunch for the two of them to eat. The pizza places in the area got to know them well too. Shawn had the corner of the break room pretty much reserved for them and none of his co-workers sat there.

He was very much into Deena as she was him. One time with fifteen minutes to spare, he walked her to the far back corner of the loading dock. Knowing his co-workers were in the break room, he told her she was all the lunch he needed. He picked her up and sat her on a skid of boxes. He couldn't help it. She was irresistible in a short dress. She whispered in a panic, afraid of getting caught.

"Trust me," he said, staring at her without blinking. It calmed her and she trusted him. He ran his hands up her thighs slightly pushing her dress up for access. He craved her and tasted her aggressively. She held his head tight and got lost in how it felt. He was spontaneous and she loved it.

He had told her he had two kids who lived in Charlotte with their mother. What he hadn't told her was that he was still married to their mother and the two of them had not even mentioned divorce. His wife was a hairstylist. She let her best friend convince her to move to Charlotte so they could open a hair salon. Shawn didn't want to move. They had no family there and starting all over was scary for him. The kids were school age and he was against uprooting them to a new unfamiliar place. He begged her to stay. She begged him to leave with her. She was sure her new business plan would be successful and made up her mind despite his pleas. She was going with or without him. She had been gone almost a year and it left him bitter. He saw his kids once in that time, having flown to Charlotte. He was sure her plan would fail and she'd come back. It hadn't failed yet as far as he knew. They agreed on the kids staying with him for Christmas and all summer while school was out, but there was still no talk of divorce. It wasn't easy to bring it up after a ten-year marriage. Shawn loved her.

But he was *in* love with Deena.

He couldn't bring himself to tell his wife about her. They still argued about her moving away. She probably would never let him see the kids again, let alone send them for Christmas and summer. He couldn't risk that. He needed to explain his situation to Deena. He knew she would understand. Or would she? She thought he was single with two kids, not married with no plans to divorce. His three-bedroom house was simply just so his kids could have enough room to run around and play. At least that's what he told her. She never questioned him. He knew she trusted him and liked him that much. He knew she *loved* him.

Shawn was content with the situation. His wife had left and he had needs. Deena was a breath of fresh air. She'd met his needs and then some. But that damn LOVE had to show up. When though? Did it squeeze itself between them during sex? Was it a third wheel on some of their dates? Had it been a part of their hours-long phone conversations? He couldn't figure it out. She *did* have the whole package.

He still had to tell her the truth. So much time had passed already that either way, he knew she wasn't going to be happy about it. To her, he was her man and that was that.

"What'd you think about us taking a trip somewhere together?"

Deena interrupted his thoughts in the middle of him chewing.

"That'd be cool. Where you wanna go? And when?"

"I don't know."

Deena couldn't hold a surprise she had any longer. It was eating at her.

The day before, she was at work listening to the

radio at her desk with the volume turned low. She heard a contest going on with who could name the characters of three family TV shows from the 80s. The call had to come in from a listener within the next half hour and the winner would get two plane tickets to fly anywhere in the U.S. Deena wanted to win the tickets for her and Shawn. It would've been an easy get away for them with a free flight. She looked around the office. Her co-worker was behind her at her desk filing her nails while talking with a customer on speaker phone. Deena's supervisor sat across the office from everyone else. She was on her phone with her head down concentrating on her note-taking. Deena whispered to her co-worker behind her that she was running to use the bathroom and she'd be back. She slipped her heels back on. She always sat barefoot at her desk to give her feet a rest.

She speeded into the bathroom and dialed the radio station. The line was busy. She stood in the mirror and waited. When she called back for the third time, she got through. She still couldn't talk loud because people walking past would hear her inside.

"Um Yes."

She was nervous.

"I'm calling in to try to win the airline tickets."

The radio DJ was loud and upbeat. Deena moved the phone away from her ear a little.

"Okay! We got our first caller!" He yelled. "What's your name?"

"Deena."

"How you doin' Deena? What side of town you callin' from?"

"The north side."

Deena smiled but her voice was quiet. She hoped she could get through the call without someone coming in the bathroom. She wished she was at home. She could be as upbeat and loud as the DJ.

"Why you sound so quiet Miss Deena? I can barely hear you." The DJ laughed. "You seriously sound like you went in the bathroom to call in."

Deena could hear the other people at the radio station laughing in the background.

"You at work? You had to sneak in the bathroom or the broom closet?"

They all laughed harder. Deena laughed too. She was embarrassed that the DJ was exactly right.

"Yeah, I'm in the bathroom at work."

She spoke up a little louder. She wanted to get the call over with and get back to her desk.

"Okay. Well let's get this going and get you back to work," the DJ said laughing.

Deena had watched lots of 80s family sit coms. She had her three favorites in mind, but the radio station chose them for the callers. She stepped inside one of the stalls. She was still nervous people might hear her from the hallway.

"Okay Miss Deena," the DJ said. He sounded a little more serious. "Name at least four characters from the following 80s sit coms: *The Facts of Life*, *The Cosby Show*, and *Family Ties.*"

Deena hadn't thought of *The Facts of Life*, but she was a guru of 80s sit coms and had binge-watched a lot of them as a teen. She left that one for last and blasted through the other two. The DJ had given her a minute and a half to finish and she did it with three seconds left. "Congratulations Miss Deena. You are correct!" He shouted. "You have won yourself a pair of airline tickets anywhere in the U.S."

The DJ told her he had to turn the call over to someone else to explain the additional details to her and where to pick up the tickets. She threw her head back and stared at the ceiling. She had been in the bathroom over ten minutes already. She almost couldn't be happy about winning for focusing on getting back to her desk in a timely manner. If her supervisor took one too many calls for her, she might've come looking for her. Someone finally picked up the line and went through a whole spiel about the airline and its promotions. Deena politely said that she had to get back to work and just needed to know where to pick up the tickets. She headed out the bathroom listening to the address being read off to her. She walked back to her desk.

"Okay thank you," she said quietly.

She looked over to her supervisor's desk. She wasn't there. Deena hung up the phone and sat back down. She planned to tell Shawn the next day.

"You talkin' about a vacation type trip?" Shawn asked.

"No. Just maybe a weekend." Deena looked at

him with dreamy eyes. "I won two airline tickets on the radio yesterday."

"For real?! How?" Shawn smiled.

Deena told him all about it and how she sneaked into the bathroom to do it.

"I didn't tell you yesterday. I wanted to surprise you today and tell you."

"That's so cool babe."

Shawn kissed her. They talked about some places they'd go for a few days, but decided to wait until after the holidays to do it. Shawn's kids were coming to visit for Christmas. He hadn't said anything about Deena meeting them.

CHAPTER 7

"**S**hit. This cannot be happening. This thing has to be defected."

Angie stared at a plus sign on a generic pregnancy test she bought after work. The directions read that the result would appear right away but it hadn't. She laid the applicator on the bathroom sink and waited. The plus sign showed after a few minutes and her stomach dropped. She walked out of the bathroom to wait a while. Maybe it *was* defected. She went back and forth to the bathroom three or four times over the next half hour. The plus sign was still there. She felt sick. No matter how much she wanted the test to be wrong, she knew it was true. She missed her last period and that never happened. It came like clock-work since she had Tia. How could she be pregnant at a time like this?! She couldn't afford to be. She still hadn't pressed Bruce about getting a job. The word JOB didn't find its way into any of their conversations. Deena helped her with two of the bills for the month. Angie knew Shawn must've still had her nose open because she gave her the money without putting in her two cents about Bruce. Anyway, it bought her some time to work extra hours at the mall kiosk so she could pay the bills for the next month. She mentioned not having the money for one of the bills due, and Bruce's response was that he thought she was going to ask for extra hours at work. It was nothing about him working at all.

She had two weeks left before money got tight again. She got even sicker thinking about it. Her head hurt. She was dizzy. She sat on the couch and hung her head down disgusted with herself. Tears hit the hard wood floor one by one.

"How could I be so stupid and let this happen?" She cried and cursed herself.

Having to tell Bruce made it all feel even worse. She replayed the comment he made about her working more hours over and over in her head. She knew he wasn't going to miraculously change his ways just because he had a child on the way. It hadn't taken him long to act like he lived alone. A child was already in the house and that selfish asshole had boldly walked in more than enough times with food and snacks for himself. Even though he shared with her, Tia always had to ask first. What son-of-a-bitch lives in the same house with a child and does that? A sharp pain pierced through Angie's forehead. She grabbed her head and squeezed, hoping it would stop pounding. For a split second, she thought about abortion. It was out of the question. She was against it, especially in this situation where two adults should've and could've been more responsible.

"Kids certainly don't ask to be born into bullshit," she said.

She cried harder and harder. She had so many emotions at once, it drove her crazy. She sobbed for several more minutes.

"Okay, get it together," she said to herself.

Tia was about to get home from school. She could take one look at Angie and know she'd been crying. Angie ran to the mirror and squeezed out any last tears. The plus sign was still there. Her heart jumped like she'd seen it for the first time. She went to the kitchen and stuffed it far down inside the trash.

"Damn. Why do I have to look so bad after I cry?"

She was back in the mirror. The whites of her eyes were completely red and her bottom eye lids always swelled at the first sign of tears. It took at least a half hour for her to look normal again after a cry. A cold towel pressed against her eyes for a few minutes might work. She couldn't think of anything else. She turned on the cold water. It was 3:02 and she went to look out the living room window. Tia's bus was there and she was getting off and running to the door. Angie had no time to work on her puffy red eyes.

She opened the door and Tia continued on inside without looking at her. She was weighed down with her bookbag and carrying a big cardboard project.

"Mama look at what I did at school."

Tia anxiously pulled off her coat and hat, excited to show Angie her work.

"I was about to ask, what's that?"

Angie thought fast on her feet and had to come up with something to tell Tia about her eyes. Tia looked up at her before she could say it.

"You been crying?"

"No. I opened a bottle of something at work and it spilled and splashed up into my face. It made my eyes burn and they're still red. They'll clear up in a little while."

"Oh. Because you sure look like you've been crying."

Tia had seen Angie cry once earlier in the year when they went to a funeral. She remembered what her eyes looked like then. She hoped Tia bought her excuse, but from her comment, she wasn't sure.

"So, what's this you got?"

Angie went right back to Tia's project, taking the attention off her eyes.

"A neighborhood. We started making our own neighborhoods and finally finished 'em today."

The cardboard had paper buildings glued down to it. Streets were drawn with marker between the buildings. Angie could make out that Tia had three houses and two buildings.

"What are these? Houses?" Angie asked, pointing to them.

"Yeah. And look, I made a hair salon and a make-up store. I told my teacher they were you're two businesses."

Tia always heard Angie talk about wishing she owned a side-by-side salon and makeup store. She had gone to one in California when she visited a friend. It had an adjoining door and one side was a full-service salon and the other was a cosmetic shop with makeup and hair products. She fell in love with the idea and pictured herself owning one. She melted knowing Tia thought about it while making her project.

"And this is our house. We live right next to your businesses mama," Tia said, still excited.

"That's my girl! That's what I'm talking about."

Angie held up a high five and Tia slapped her hand against it smiling. Angie kept smiling but felt bad about always saying what she wanted and never trying to go after it. She procrastinated going back to school. She had to do that first before she could run a successful business, not to mention saving the money to even be able to open one. She sure had her own little cheerleader in Tia to root her on.

"My own daughter really thinks we're gonna have this one day," she thought to herself.

She wasn't sure if she could pull it off so it was always nothing more than a vision. Had she talked about it that much that Tia believed she was actually going to have it? Angie didn't want Tia thinking this was something that could or would happen soon since she built it into existence on a piece of cardboard.

"Now you know that's gonna take a while for me to get," Angie said. "I have to go back to school first and then save the money for it. So, it's not gonna happen anytime soon, okay?"

"Okay," Tia said.

Angie wasn't sure if Tia cared one way or the other, but wanted to make sure she understood there was a process to having something, and it wasn't as easy as making it out of paper in a school project. It was too much to think about at the moment. She couldn't handle being overwhelmed. It was why she was such a procrastinator. She wanted everything in arm's reach and easy to get. She could jump small hurdles to get by, but if anything seemed too big to handle, she easily dismissed it.

She stared at Tia's project. She wasn't even close to making it a reality. The rent was a struggle and she wasn't getting enough hours at work to stay above water.

"I wanna hang it in my room," Tia said.

She picked up the cardboard by one end and walked into her bedroom.

"Just put it against the wall for now and I'll see if I can find some nails to hang it up later."

Instead of Tia's project making Angie happy, it brought her right back to a place she was becoming familiar with---being depressed. She looked at the trash can where she stuffed the pregnancy test. She composed herself from coming to tears again. Another baby definitely meant her own business was out of the question. What scared her most was what Bruce's reaction would be. She hadn't heard from him all day but planned to tell him right away. She just had to hold off until it was official. She called the doctor to make an appointment for the next morning and she just had to get through the night. Maybe it was a false alarm.

CHAPTER 8

The kids were coming. Shawn was on his way to pick them up from the airport. It was the first time they'd been home in a year. He was excited to see them. His wife told him about airport escorts who rode with kids on their flight and saw them to their final destinations. It was a little extra added to each ticket for the service. He had never heard of it. That way, she wouldn't have to pay for an extra ticket and fly with them. She had finally given in to letting them stay with him for Christmas break. After a few arguments and Shawn complaining about her not letting them come for the summer, she agreed. He still couldn't get over how unfair she'd been the whole time. She could do what she wanted but when it came to the kids, he wasn't going to stand for her not holding up her end of the deal.

They loved Christmas time. What kid didn't? Shawn planned plenty to do in the next two weeks. There was a tree lighting downtown and trolley rides with Santa Claus. It was a winter fest by the pier with indoor rides and games. He couldn't stand the outdoor stuff because of the cold. But he wanted the kids to have fun, especially since this wasn't their usual

Christmas with all of them as a family. It would be different, but they'd love it. He had already bought them a bunch of gifts and they could open one every other day until Christmas. He smiled thinking about it. He missed them so much.

Wreaths and ribbons decorated the poles and bench seats along the airport entrance. Lights trimmed the skywalks and underpasses off the freeway exit. The airport escort was bringing the kids to the baggage claim doors to wait for him so he didn't have to park the car and go inside. He drove toward the baggage claim lane. Cars were stopped at each exit door. He could see the Delta sign ahead, but traffic was at a standstill. He was irritated. While he knew his kids were with an adult, it was still an adult they didn't know. He wanted to get to them as quick as he could. Ten minutes went by and his car hadn't moved. He could have left the car and walked to the Delta exit in less time. At least the kids would be with him in the car. He wondered if the escort thought he wasn't coming and took the kids back inside. He was not up for a wild goose chase for his kids through the airport. Just as he was about to turn on his hazard lights and shut the car off to run to the Delta exit, a sheriff's deputy flashed his squad car lights and got the traffic moving.

"It's about damn time!" Shawn shouted to himself out loud in the car.

After a few more minutes with the traffic moving, he drove up to the Delta baggage claim. He saw that the kids were with a woman. She had to be the airport escort, so he grabbed for his driver's license in his wallet right away. He had to show that he was the person authorized to pick them up. The kids saw him pulling up and ran to the car.

"Daddy!" They both yelled.

As he stepped out of the car and walked around to the sidewalk, the woman reached down to pick up their bags and carry them to the car. She wasn't waiting for Shawn to approach her with his identification. The kids wrapped themselves around his legs, excited to see him. The woman walked toward him holding luggage in each of her hands. It was his wife.

Shawn felt like he was punched in the stomach. She didn't just fly with the kids, nixing the escort at the last minute. She had luggage. She was staying. He couldn't say a word. His mouth wouldn't open. He stared at her with a confused look. She spoke first and told him in a much embarrassing way that she was back for good. She and her best friend turned business partner couldn't agree on things from day one. She criticized herself for not realizing that before moving away. She had only stuck it out that long to save face and not have Shawn and everyone else tell her about how they knew she made a mistake. But one last argument and her friend's dominating personality sent her packing. She bought a last-minute plane ticket to fly with the kids.

Shawn still stared at her while she talked. He looked at the cars stopping ahead and the people coming and going. He wasn't sure how to feel. A small part of him wanted to be happy to see her, but his mind went straight to Deena. He told her the kids were coming for Christmas break. He finally told her he wanted her to meet them, but he hadn't come up with a way for that to happen. He still hadn't told her he was married. Now he wasn't sure at all about how to handle any of this. His mind raced thinking about it. A car horn blew and snapped him out of it. His wife had walked past him and she and the kids got into the car. Cars were lining up behind his, and some managed to maneuver around it to pick up people. Now *he* was one of the people holding up the traffic. He grabbed up the rest of the luggage and loaded it into the car. The sheriff's deputy was moving around the traffic again at the end of the line. Shawn jumped into the driver's seat and quickly blended in with the other cars to leave the airport.

⟫◈⟪

Deena was on the other side of town spending some well overdue time with her grandmother. Accompanying her to the doctor had been resorted to a phone call every now and then. Shawn had taken up most of her time since they met. Her grandmother noticed right away. One day when Deena called she asked in the only way a grandmother could.

"So, who's courtin you?"

Deena couldn't believe it and tried to play dumb.

"What'd you mean by that?"

"When you're smitten with somebody, you forget who everybody else is."

She knew exactly why Deena hadn't been around.

Deena was embarrassed and laughed without saying a word. She knew Shawn's kids were flying in and he'd be spending the day with them. She had promised her grandmother she would come and take her to visit an old friend of hers who was sick in the hospital. They ran a few errands afterwards and she stopped at Buddy Squirrel to get her grandmother's favorite caramel and cheese popcorn. She told her to wait in the car while she ran inside to get it. She made a quick call to Shawn to see how his day was going with the kids, but he didn't answer. He always answered the phone, but she figured he must've been busy at the moment. She left a message and walked back to the car with the popcorn.

It was 7PM. An hour had passed in between Deena leaving Shawn the message and dropping off her grandmother. She called him again on her way home. His phone went straight to voicemail. She hung up and called right back. Voicemail again. She left another message.

"Hey, it's me. Call me as soon as you get this. I called you a few times and I'm just getting your voicemail. Hope everything is okay. Love you."

Deena worried.

Shawn always answered his phone for her. He would've at least called back by now. She was tempted to drive by his house but didn't. He wanted to introduce her to his kids, not have her meet them by her popping up at the door unannounced. She went home and waited for him to call. Hopefully nothing happened and he'd call soon saying something was wrong with his phone or even that he'd lost it somewhere. Hopefully.

She woke up to the Ninja air fryer infomercial on TV. It was 5:47AM and the regular TV programs were off the air. She had fallen asleep on her couch. She grabbed for her phone. Shawn hadn't called at all. Her heart beat fast and worry came over her even more. What could've happened? Did something happen? She called again and got the voicemail.

"Shawn, oh my God. What is going on? I have not heard from you and I'm worried."

She paused for a second wanting to go on, but hung up. If he didn't have his phone, how would he get the messages anyway? Something had to happen. Was it a bad car accident? Did something happen to one of the kids or did the house catch on fire? Her mind raced trying to figure it out. She jumped off the couch and ran to the bathroom to fluff out the side of her hair that was flattened while she was asleep. She grabbed her car keys and phone and darted out the door, headed to his house. She couldn't care about how he took it, and she'd apologize later.

The cul-de-sac where he lived was quiet and

from the snow falling overnight, she could see that her car was the first to drive into it. There were no other tire tracks. His house was dead center and had a red front door. It could be seen from the other end of the block that led up to it.

Seeing the red door sunk Deena's stomach. She had been driving fast to get there, but now it seemed like her car crawled up to the house. No footprints had graced the doorstep and the blinds were all closed. She sat in the car staring at the house for several minutes, contemplating going to the door. What if he didn't answer? Deena suddenly realized she had never met anyone in Shawn's family since they'd been dating. She wouldn't know how to contact them to find out if anyone had seen or heard from him. It was Sunday so she'd have to wait the day out and see if he'd show up to work the next day.

"Oh my God that's right. He's on vacation," she said out loud.

She remembered he took off the week leading up to Christmas. The company was closed on Christmas Day. She stared at the door still thinking. Something told her he wasn't going to answer. If that were the case, she'd have to sit out there and wait to see if he'd show up or come back and try again. She was so nervous her hands shook. Staring at the door, she reached for her purse and got her phone out. She made one last call to him and flung it on the seat after hearing the voicemail again. She got out of the car not bothering to see where it landed. Snow covered the tops of her shoes and she dashed up to the front door and pushed the bell. Shawn woke up early even on his off days, so a ringing doorbell wouldn't interrupt his sleep. If he was there, it wouldn't take him long to get to the door. She gave it a couple of minutes and rang the bell again. She started to feel the cold of the snow covering her shoes. She wanted to scream his name out loud and yell at the windows like a crazy person but she couldn't. The cul-de-sac was so quiet a rabbit could probably be heard running through the snow. Not a soul had come out or driven through there since she came. She had to go back to her car and figure out what to do next. She turned to walk away from the door and it opened.

It was Shawn's wife. *She* had obviously been woken up by the doorbell. Her ponytail-like bun bopped around on top of her head and she was wearing a long shirt gown and slippers. She had thrust the inside door open quick and squinted, trying to focus on Deena. Deena looked back at her and frowned, expecting to see Shawn inside the door. Her thoughts raced for a second and scattered in her head.

Who was this? Where was Shawn? She knew she had the right house but why had she come face-to-face with a woman who had apparently spent the night there?

"Umm," Deena said to let on that she was obviously confused. "Is Shawn here?"

"He's still asleep."

His wife started to show a subtle frown, not sure if Deena was a bill collector or salesperson showing up that early. Clearly, she was a woman asking for Shawn and Shawn only. She wasn't dressed the part either.

"Who are you?" His wife asked.

Deena didn't realize she was frozen in place. She had a much different process going through her head about who was standing in front of her. She was relieved to hear Shawn was asleep and not somewhere decapitated. But who was this? She had been with Shawn for six months now and thought this woman had to be his sister or cousin who'd stayed overnight answering the door in a nightgown.

"I'm his girlfriend."

"Girlfriend?!"

Shawn's wife had raised her voice in shock. Her eyes opened wide.

"Well how long have you been his *girlfriend*, because I'm his wife."

She might as well have gotten in a car and drove it right over Deena because it's what she felt like hearing those words. She instantly went numb.

Wife? She couldn't compete with a wife. She tried to process what she was hearing. For a second, she was broken but she refused to show it.

"Well you must've been on a six-month vacation from your marriage because that's how long it's been." Deena spoke up to keep her voice from cracking.

A knot formed in her throat and she knew if she

stood there any longer, the tears would come. Before Shawn's wife could say her next word, Deena cut her off.

"So, I'm not gonna waste my breath saying tell Shawn not to call me again because he obviously already decided that, which is why I'm here. I didn't hear from him all yesterday evening." She spoke quick and pierced her eyes at her. "But tell him the next time he decides to have a girlfriend on the side, he may wanna think about it first before he fucks over the wrong person."

She walked back to her car as fast as her feet could carry her. She almost made a new trail, only overlapping a few of her first steps up to the door. More snow covered her shoes but she didn't feel the cold anymore. Humiliation was all she could feel and she made it back to the car just as tears painted her face. She left the cul-de-sac not bothering to look at the red door again to see if it closed behind her. She turned the car onto the next block and pulled over. Her hand shook holding the gear shift but she slammed it in park. She threw her head against the steering wheel and let out a good cry.

CHAPTER 9

I t was New Year's Eve. Angie was on her third glass of sparkling grape juice. She smiled at Tia's Barbie cup on the coffee table filled with some. She let her stay up late to bring in the New Year. They played at least fifteen games of checkers. It was Tia's favorite game. Angie stared at her curled up on the couch asleep. She had been watching the night's music shows on TV. For the first time in the past four years, Angie didn't go out. Being pregnant and alone depressed her. Once she mentioned it to Bruce, he pretended to be happy, but days later, packed his stuff and left while she was at work. He left her a voicemail message saying he wasn't ready for kids and wasn't the "family man" type. He added that he only hoped she considered an abortion. The word *sorry* for his irresponsible decision was nowhere in the message. And he had the nerve to suggest abortion, but didn't bother to say he'd offer up any money for one. Angie screamed and threw the phone clear across the room after she listened to it. She went around the apartment looking for anything he might've left behind. It was going to the bottom of the trash can and she would've suddenly got in the mood to clean out the refrigerator and dump expired food on top of it. It would've made her feel better to take out some rage on something, but he had taken every stitch of what he owned. Not even a dirty sock was lying around.

She still hadn't told anyone she was pregnant. She was too busy trying to figure out how she was going to manage it financially. And deep down inside, she was embarrassed.

The phone rang. Angie knew it was somebody calling to say Happy New Year.

"Hello."

"Happy New Year!" It was her cousin Kayla.

"Happy New Year." She pretended to sound like she was smiling.

"What's going on? It's awfully quiet in the background, and I didn't even think you'd be home."

Kayla knew Angie never had a dull New Year's Eve. Angie could hear loud music in the background and people talking. Kayla was obviously at a party. She never had a dull New Year's Eve either.

"Yeah, I'm at home this year. Me and Tia brought the new year in together." Angie giggled. "Well, I brought it in by myself. She fell asleep on me like a half hour ago."

"Oh. Brian's mother couldn't watch her for you?"

"I just wasn't in the party mood this year. My money is tight."

Angie left it at that. She didn't want to add pregnant and alone. Kayla and Angie were close and

Angie could tell her about everything, but this was not the time to have that conversation.

"Where are you?"

She wanted to keep Kayla from asking her anything more.

"I'm with Derrick. His uncle had a party this year so that's where we ended up."

Kayla had been with her boyfriend Derrick for six years. He was no different than Bruce. He just managed to stick around. Or at least Kayla hadn't managed to kick him loose. She was rough around the edges and didn't seem to mind putting up with the drama that came with a man like that. She once caught him in a bar feeling up a woman with his hand up her dress. She sat right next to them in the booth, grabbed one of the woman's boobs and squeezed saying, "Bitch, get your own man!" She gave Derrick a couple of fist blows to the face and walked out. He didn't end up at home that night, but they were back together in the next few days. Kayla was clearly his meal ticket. He couldn't stay away. She liked the no job, bad boy type, but times ten. She felt like she controlled the relationship if she took care of the man. He couldn't leave if he had nowhere else to go. Most people call that stupid. Angie knew she couldn't judge her. She hadn't come to her senses about Bruce. If he wouldn't have left on his own, he probably would've been there ringing in the New Year with her.

Kayla was happy-go-lucky. She never acted like

things bothered her. She was always up for a good time and Angie could always count on her for a pick-me-up. She had Angie's back and it was never a better time that she needed cheering up. But she wasn't going to ruin Kayla's night with bad news. Kayla had only met Bruce a couple of times. That was because he and Angie stayed holed up in the house for much of their short run of a relationship.

Kayla hadn't asked about him. It had to be the drinks. Angie talked fast and rushed her off the phone before she could.

"Well, have fun and don't drink too much. I'll call you tomorrow to see how the rest of your night went."

"Okay. I'm on my third drink, but I'm done after one more. Don't worry. Talk you to later. Happy New Year again."

"Happy New Year. Bye."

Angie was relieved she didn't ask about Bruce. She would've burst into the biggest ugly cry. She hadn't forgiven herself yet. It had been two months but she was far from over it. She watched another hour of TV to take her mind off of it. She took Tia's princess comforter from her bed and laid it over her while she slept. She got on the other couch across from her and finally fell asleep.

Deena and Angie hadn't spoken in a few weeks. They had both been in depressed stupors and didn't want to talk to anyone. Deena seemed to be having a harder time. She had called in sick to work for a week and then requested two weeks of her next year's vacations saying she was dealing with a personal matter. She hadn't left the house and barely left the bed. She even canceled her hair appointment. Other than a call or two from her grandmother, she didn't answer the phone for anyone else. Shawn wasn't one of the calls. He never bothered to call and explain or apologize for being a heartless asshole. That hurt her the most.

She finally got up the strength to call Angie. She had to vent and curse Shawn to someone other than herself. It would help her feel better.

She started right in when Angie answered.

"That motherfucker is married."

"Huh?! Deena?"

"Angie, he is married." Deena couldn't help it and the tears flowed.

"Shawn? How do you know? What happened?"

"Apparently his wife reappeared from somewhere or the bitch came back from the dead or something. I don't know."

"Are you serious?!"

"He told me his kids were coming in town and he was picking 'em up from the airport. I didn't hear from him all day and was calling and calling. I went to his house the next morning thinking something happened to him and she answered the door."

Deena cried harder talking about it. Angie tried to make sense of what she was saying through her mumbled words.

"So, you hadn't heard from him all day and he was supposed to be picking up his kids?"

"Yeah."

"And the next day he still didn't call so you went to his house and his wife answered the door?"

"Yeah. How could I not have known all this time?" Deena couldn't stop crying.

"Oh my God, that's crazy."

Angie got upset hearing Deena force out words through tears.

"And he still hasn't called you?"

"No. I don't even wanna talk to him right now. It hurts more that he didn't bother to answer my calls all that day and say something then. Here I was thinking he was hurt or something, and it never dawned on me that was the case."

Deena wasn't crying as hard anymore.

"So, what did she say?"

"Asked me who I was and I told her. I'm his girlfriend. And that's when she said she was his wife. I asked her was she on a fuckin' six-month vacation because that's how long it's been and he never mentioned having a wife."

"And what'd she say?"

"Nothin. I told her to tell him he'd better watch who he fucks over the next time."

"I can't believe that. But you had been to his

house a bunch of times right? She never came around all that time, so they must've been separated and got back together or somethin."

Angie tried to piece together what could've been the case. It didn't make sense to her either how Shawn could date Deena all that time and his wife not be around.

"That could be the only reason for that. Especially with the kids not being there either. They probably decided to get back together and he didn't tell you."

"All he said was that he had two kids and they lived in North Carolina with their mother. I should've known he couldn't own a three-bedroom house in the suburbs as a single person working at Dooner Sausage." Deena rambled on. "And I can't stop thinking about being in that house. How do you just bring a woman into another woman's house? That's the worst part of this. I wanna be told the situation and then make the decision on my own to be in somebody else's house. He's a coward bastard that wanted to get his sex on and play around a while until his wife got back. I just had to be the dumb ass that fell for him."

"Don't say that about yourself. That's his loss. I never would've guessed you'd call me and say that. That's so hard to believe."

"I'm just sick about it. I haven't been eating and I'm losing weight. I loved him to death."

"Why didn't you call me sooner? You've been dealing with it all this time by yourself?"

Angie was focused on Deena and it made her forget her own problems for a minute. She hadn't called her with her issues either and this wasn't the time to bring them up. Deena was a mess and she didn't want to turn the conversation around and make it about her instead. She definitely had to wait until Deena was over this well enough.

"I just didn't wanna talk to anybody. You're the first person I'm telling. Well you're the only person that knew about us really. Except for a couple of the girls I work with."

"Well you gotta get outta that house and take your mind off of that for a while. You'll drive yourself crazy. You wanna come over here?"

"No. I don't really feel like doing anything. I wish I could get up the nerve to go to his house and throw a brick through his car window."

"I'm glad you said *wish*. Don't get up the nerve. And if you do, call me so I can stop you."

Angie knew that wasn't Deena's style, but she could tell she was mad enough to actually do it.

"He has to pay for what he did. He put out the best sex ever, told me he loved me every day, and fucked me over in the end."

"You don't think he really loved you and just didn't tell you he was married?"

Angie still couldn't believe a man could tell a woman over and over that he loved her and be exclusive with her for six months without actually feeling something for her.

"Apparently not. I haven't heard from him. And you don't do that to somebody you claim to love."

"Well I get it. I'm just a little confused."

"Now I see why I can't find a decent man. It's none out there. All of 'em are shitty in some way or another."

"Tell me about it. I…" Angie stopped.

She wanted to second that thinking about Bruce and how he ran off but she caught herself. This was Deena's moment, not hers. She had to let her vent. And that Deena did. They talked for the next two hours and Deena had even cried again. She couldn't stop thinking about Shawn and how much she missed him and hated him at the same time. Angie silently cried with her, relating to her own situation but for a totally different reason. She had a baby on the way and the father was probably nowhere to be found. She did her best to console Deena until they said their goodbyes. Her turn would come in due time to cry on her shoulder.

CHAPTER 10

Deena stared at the two plane tickets she won from the radio station. She decided she couldn't take the agony anymore of thinking about Shawn and all the things they did together. She cried after driving past the pizza place they ordered from on their lunch breaks. She couldn't even look over at Dooner Sausage after getting to work. She started coming from another direction on the side street of Ward's to get to the parking garage so she could avoid it. Almost everything made her think of him.

Her aunt and uncle from Georgia had come to visit her grandmother recently and Deena inquired about living there. She said she wanted a "change of scenery" and should move there to start over. They told her she'd be welcome there and they'd help her until she got a job. She had management experience in retail and knew it wouldn't be hard to find work. At least one of the plane tickets wouldn't go to waste.

She booked a flight for that next month.

Everything moved so fast from that point. She didn't give herself time to think about anything. She only focused on leaving and it became a quick way to clear her head. She still couldn't get anything past her grandmother who knew exactly what she was up to. She had never shared the details of her love life with her grandmother at all, but endured the talks from her about not letting a man run her away from everything she's always known. Deena loved and hated her grandmother's wisdom but she wasn't about to share the Shawn blues with her. She was too embarrassed about it and didn't want to hear her lectures about men. They had talked twice since Deena decided to move and both times her grandmother managed to sneak 'Don't leave home over a man, 'cause you still won't be happy,' into the conversation. Deena would only say she didn't like her job anymore or she's always wanted to live somewhere else and try something new. Her grandmother listened patiently to everything she said, but without question got the last word with, 'Okay, you heard what I said though.'

Deena plunged on ignoring any advice against it. She knew it was sudden and irrational, but a quick fix.

————))(((————

Angie didn't take Deena's news well. Maybe one of the reasons was because Deena called her at 7AM to break it to her. Angie forced her crusted eyes open wider to answer the phone. It had to be an emergency. Deena never called her that early.

"Hello."

Angie tried to sound more awake than she really was.

"Hey, I called to tell you I'm moving out of town."

Deena held the phone out from her own ear waiting for Angie to yell something. She purposely called her that early to say it bluntly and get it over with. She didn't know how else to tell her.

"Huh?" Angie wasn't sure if she heard her correctly. "You're doing what?"

"I'm moving out of town."

"Why and where?"

Angie was more awake and was irritated with Deena's abrupt decision. Her straight forward and stern tone let Deena know she wasn't happy with her. Seven o'clock didn't help the situation either.

"Georgia. I just don't wanna live here anymore."

"Don't tell me you're letting Shawn get to you that much."

"Yeah, I'm letting Shawn get to me that much."

Deena felt silly having to admit to her weakness. She could be honest with Angie because Angie knew her best.

"I just need to get away for a while."

"Who lives in Georgia?"

"My aunt and uncle. They said I can stay with them until I get a job and my own place."

"What is moving away gonna do? I don't want you to go."

Angie's voice was still stern. She was upset.

71

Deena always fell hard for guys, which was why she had only been in a few serious relationships. But Angie knew her friend to be resilient to any and everything. Why was this getting her down so much? Deena had always told her she made bad choices in men, but while she made so called "good" ones, was she just embarrassed that she got duped? Or had she fallen so hard this time it caused her to up and leave?

Angie couldn't help asking.

"Are you embarrassed about what happened or were just *that* in love? Because you never had a problem telling me about how you thought the guys in my life were no good for me. So, is that it? You fell for one in disguise that lied to you the whole time?"

"No. And I'm sorry for all that. I for sure can't talk about you and nobody you've been with. But yes, I was just *that* in love and I'm mad at myself. I have to get that out of my head and the only way I know how to do it is to leave for a while. I may come back in a couple of years, but right now I gotta get away."

Angie told Deena she was pregnant. She didn't waste any time getting it out. It was even more frustrating for her hearing Deena say she was leaving and she hadn't got the chance to tell her until that moment. She didn't hide the fact that Bruce left the minute she told him.

"What! When did you find out?"

"Last month. I didn't get my period and I knew right away. It comes like clock-work."

"Why are you just now telling me? And Bruce left?!"

Deena didn't know what answer she wanted first. She and her best friend had both gone through something at the same time but she knew Angie was in worst shape.

"I wanted to get to the doctor first to make sure I really was," Angie explained. I did and found out I'm due in August. I told Bruce and a few days later I came home and all his shit was gone. I haven't heard from him since and stopped trying to get in touch with him."

She said this quick and in a straight forward matter-of-fact way. She had already started to get over it, talking without getting teary eyed.

"Wait a minute. All this happened basically a month ago? Why didn't you tell me? What are you gonna do?"

Deena couldn't get her thoughts together fast enough. How could Angie just say it like that and not bat an eye?

"Girl, I've cried my eyes out enough over it. I've banged my fist against stuff around here. I've screamed out loud. Let's see. What else have I done?"

Angie paused like she was thinking.

"And Bruce upped and left?"

"Yup. Fuck him."

"I don't even know what to say."

"Say you told me to drop him a long time ago and I didn't get it through my stupid ass brain."

A big part of her knew even though Deena had been duped herself, she had still been right about Bruce all along.

"I got myself into this mess so I gotta deal with it."

"Well, like I said, I'm sorry for that. I should've been paying attention to my own situation and I would've seen the signs."

"Do you *have* to go?" Angie cut her off.

It was the worse time for her to move away. They had been friends since freshman year in high school and knew everything about each other. She needed her friend to stay. Deena felt bad for leaving, especially at that time. They had been through a lot together.

"I already gave my two-week notice at work, told my landlord I'm moving, and I'm putting my stuff in storage until I can get it all down there."

Deena tried to put it as if she couldn't reverse her decision. Too much had been done and the plans had to carry on. She didn't want to think about staying. Her mind was made up. She reassured Angie that she was just a phone call away and they'd still talk as much as usual.

"It won't even seem like I'm gone. It's just my aunt and uncle there so you know I'm gonna call you to get me through the boredom."

Angie thought about her pregnancy with Tia and having Deena around. She sure wouldn't need to talk about her own boredom. She needed help getting through much more than that. Deena promised her she'd come back and stay a few days when the baby was born.

⸻ ⟨◉⟩ ⸻

Angie still managed to pull in extra hours at work a month later. A girl who worked the evening shift quit and she took those hours a few times a week. Her baby bump wasn't starting to show yet, but morning sickness was not out of the picture. It wasn't even sticking to its "morning" schedule. She had the mall security guard who stood nearby the kiosk to watch it while she ran to the nearest bathroom to vomit her guts at least once during her shift. The extra money helped her catch up and maintain the bills, but she still hadn't told her supervisor she was pregnant. She worried about having to pay for day care when she returned to work. Tia wasn't an issue. She was in school all day and when Angie worked evenings, she went to her dad's house.

This new baby coming threw a monkey wrench into everything. Making $10.90 an hour just wouldn't cut it with a new addition to the family. Formula and diapers had gone up since Tia was a baby. It wasn't something she had to worry much about at the time because Tia's father hadn't run off like a pussy coward. She wished she would've told Bruce to go about his business the day he came back to her apartment after taking her to sign up for the job training. It was clear as day to her now that he only needed a place to stay.

She got some help from Kayla without Kayla knowing it. She had borrowed Angie's car for a couple of days. Hers was in the shop. She had taken the days off work, but needed to run errands. She told Angie she'd fill it up with gas and make sure she got her to and from work. Angie still hadn't told her she was pregnant. She gladly let her borrow her car because it meant free gas and extra money in her pocket.

CHAPTER 11

The weather was much nicer in Georgia. Wearing a jacket in February couldn't be beat. Light flurries of snow usually shut the cities down and people took to their homes as if a tornado, earthquake, and tsunami hit them all at once. The scenery was much different from anywhere in the Midwest. The city scene for what Deena was used to quickly dissolved into the country side and streets turned into roads with dirt and green landscapes fighting for space. Neighbors were anywhere from a hundred feet to a half mile away from each other. Any and everyone who had something remotely close to a front porch sat on it in the morning and sometimes all day.

Deena saw the small town as peaceful, but it didn't take long for boredom to set in. Her uncle drove her around and showed her that her new hometown was all within a twenty-block square with only two stores. The nearest mall was at least forty-five minutes away. That meant the nearest job was the same distance. Deena tried not to think about it and kept her focus on clearing her mind and making the best of a new place.

It wasn't a good start. The house was a small two-bedroom with mix match furniture and creaky hardwood floors. Most houses in the south didn't have basements so there was nowhere to go to escape everyone else for a while. Deena stayed confined to the bedroom most of the time. It kept her out of sight and out of the way. She knew two people could be comfortable in such a small place, but a third moving in was just *wrong*. However, there were some positives to her new stay. Her aunt cooked breakfast every morning and the smell was an alarm clock. Deena woke up inhaling sweet and savory aromas of pancakes, bacon and eggs or sausage, grits, and biscuits with gravy. Salmon croquettes were a Sunday specialty. The little house was its own tiny Cracker Barrel restaurant. Anyone could appreciate that. There was also every cable channel on the living room TV, the only one in the house. Her aunt and uncle left for work every morning after breakfast and Deena took advantage of the alone time all day curled up on the couch watching everything from old episodes of *Three's Company* to Wesley Snipes in *New Jack City.*

Two months went by before she got a job. She had to wait until weekends to use her aunt and uncle's car for the forty-five-minute drive to the mall to fill out applications. She took a job at a shoe store working evenings. A sales clerk was far from what her position was at Ward's, but it was something. Sharing the car with her aunt and uncle was the plan until she could save the ridiculous amount of money it cost to have hers brought there by flatbed truck. She only saw her aunt and uncle for those morning breakfasts and her off days. They went to bed at nine every night and except for the creaky floors, the house was quiet when Deena got home. She channel surfed at night and talked to Angie on the phone more than ever to overcome any moments of thinking about Shawn. It never failed that he popped up in her mind somehow. The love scenes on TV always did it and Deena cursed him to herself.

"That motherfuckin coward asshole. And who is that bitch of his that just reappeared? Who was she out fucking for six months and decided she wanted him back all of a sudden?"

The scene of Shawn's wife answering the door replayed in her head. She picked up the phone and called Angie.

"What's up country girl?"

"Don't call me that," Deena said.

"Well isn't that what you become when you live in the deep, deep south in a town that you can see all of just by spinning around in a circle?" Angie joked. "You know you just need to come back. That is not a good fit for you."

"It's working out," Deena said, trying to convince herself that she wasn't homesick. "What you up to?"

"Nothin. We haven't talked in a couple of days. I ended up telling crazy Kayla I'm pregnant and that Bruce is M.I.A."

"Oh boy. What did she say?" You know your cousin has issues," Deena laughed.

"She lost it. Asking if I was sure I didn't know where he was so she could find him and curse him out."

"And you know she will too."

"I don't think he left town. I'm pretty sure he's still around somewhere laying low hoping he doesn't run into me."

"Yeah I'm sure he is," Deena agreed sourly. "But I thought you would've run into him somewhere by now."

"Me too. And I don't think he had the money like that to up and leave. Besides, he doesn't have to leave town to avoid being a daddy."

"When is your appointment?" Deena asked.

It was time for Angie to find out the sex of the baby.

"In two more days. I hope it's a boy."

She had had enough of the pink craze from Tia, and at times it drove her a little crazy. She could use some blues and greens in her life. She put her hand over her baby bump and rubbed.

"You just have to be a boy," she said to herself.

"Where's Tia?" Deena asked.

"With her dad. You know he's got a baby on the way?"

Angie sounded dry. She didn't particularly care for him landing a solid relationship and getting himself a family. Here she was with a baby on the way and still single, struggling to make ends meet. How had he been so lucky and not her?

"No!" Deena quietly shouted, so not to wake her aunt and uncle. "Him and his girlfriend?"

"Yeah. Tia came home the other day and told me. She said, 'Guess what? My daddy and Tiffany are having a baby too. Now I'm gonna have two brothers or two sisters at the same time.'" She imitated Tia's kid voice.

Deena could hear that she was irritated and laughed.

"That's so weird. Why you sound like that? You don't wanna be pregnant at the same time as Brian's fiancee?" Deena kept giggling.

She knew Angie didn't like the thought of it.

"No. I don't but I'm due in August anyway. Long before her so it really doesn't matter." Angie tried to make herself feel better. "I just don't want Tia going around saying her mom and "stepmom" are pregnant. You know some people will get the wrong impression. Thinking her dad got both of us pregnant."

"Oh, girl please. You worry about the silliest things. People will *not* think that. And anyway, who cares what people think?! They don't know the situation."

"You know it's so many stupid people out there and today people don't think it's the way it really is. Today the first thing they think is the man was sleeping with both his ex and his current at the same time and got 'em both pregnant."

Angie tried to convince Deena that it was really what bothered her about the whole thing. But she was secretly jealous of Brian. Deena ranted on about how ridiculous she sounded and Angie was surprised that she never caught on to the real reason. Deena knew her better than she knew herself sometimes.

———◦《◉》◦———

Angie went in for her appointment two days later. She laid on the exam table watching the technician glove up to start her ultrasound. She was used to being alone by now through this. She got through things imagining a husband with her all the time. That's how it was supposed to be. She wasn't alone with Tia. Why now? Dealing with it all had become the norm for her but August was around the corner. She couldn't think about her delivery and having no one there. Just having anyone wouldn't work either. Deena *had* to come back before the baby was born. Kayla always had her back too, but she would get on her nerves, not to mention embarrass her. She was definitely not someone to have around when bringing a baby into the world.

"Ready?"

The technician was standing over her holding the belly tool with gobs of clear gel on top of it. Angie snapped herself out of it and focused her attention on the pair of hands over her baby bump.

"Yeah, I'm ready."

The technician told her to watch the monitor for the baby.

"Yeah I know how this works. I have a daughter," Angie said with a half-smile.

The gel was warm on her belly as the technician rolled the tool around and pressed down in certain spots. Things looked garbled and unclear on the monitor. How did people know what they were looking at? She sure didn't. All she could make out was the head. The rest of the baby's body looked like a badly drawn kindergarten picture. She didn't know what the arms or legs or anything was. The technician rolled the tool and pressed and pressed. She had to get more gel.

"I'm having trouble getting the sex," the technician said, staring at the monitor. "The baby is in a weird position."

"What type of position?"

"See the baby has its legs up toward its chest."

The technician pointed to the monitor showing her. Angie had no idea what she was looking at.

"Yeah."

She agreed and didn't let on that she didn't know the baby's legs from its arms from its butt. The technician apologized and told her she'd have to schedule a second ultrasound to find out the baby's sex. She reminded her that her insurance didn't cover a second one and she'd have to pay out of pocket. Three hundred dollars wasn't just lying around for Angie to use on a second try. She slid the ultrasound picture in her purse and walked out of the clinic. It was going to bug her not knowing what she was having. Her small baby bump poked through a black t-shirt she wore. Maternity clothes would be more comfortable but money was tight as usual. She pulled her pea coat together around her stomach and buttoned it, hurrying to her car. Kayla had called wanting to borrow it again.

She didn't mind putting up with her sometimes. At least she'd fill the tank up before returning it. Kayla always claimed her and Derrick's car was in the shop. Angie had her share of car troubles with the many lemons she had so she made it her business to keep a nicer car with a car note in the budget just to have something reliable.

Kayla ran out to the car as soon as Angie pulled up.

"You must've been standing in the window lookin' out. I didn't even get to park the car good yet."

Angie had never seen Kayla in such a hurry.

"I was lookin' out. Me and Derrick have to be somewhere."

Kayla was still putting her coat on and looked panicked. Angie usually let her drive her to work so she was getting out to walk over to the passenger seat. Derrick came running out the front door talking on his cell phone and jumped in the back seat.

"Girl please hurry up." Kayla rushed Angie out of the driver seat.

"What's the damn hurry! Shit. I'm pregnant."

Angie wanted to know what the issue was that she was all of a sudden being rushed to loan out her own car.

"We were just supposed to be somewhere a half hour ago. I'm sorry. Thanks for letting us use the car."

Kayla pretended to slow herself down and be appreciative. Angie stepped carefully to sit herself in the front seat. She was so not pleased with the situation. Kayla avoided the question about where they needed to be and Derrick was secretive in the back seat on his cell phone.

"Man, I can't talk right now. I'll see you in a minute," he said as he hung up his phone. He hadn't even spoken to Angie.

"My doctor's appointment ran a little over. That's what took me a while to get here," Angie said, letting it show that she was irritated.

Kayla drove over the speed limit and came to stops at the lights inching past the crosswalk line, impatient for the green. She concentrated hard on the cars around her and didn't seem to be listening.

"That's okay. We'll get there," she said quickly.

Angie thought about where the hell they needed to be and what was so secretive about it? She groaned heavy closing her eyes. She pressed one side of her stomach and her head went down slowly toward her chest. The baby was moving around. Angie wondered if it was the situation and the hectic car ride. It had to be the tension. She read that babies can sense things from the womb. She groaned again as Kayla was pulling into the mall parking lot to drop her off.

"You alright? You gonna be able to stay at work?" Kayla asked, stopping fast at the entrance.

Angie reached for the door handle to open it.

"Yup, I'm good. The baby's just kicking. I'm sure it's from your crazy ass driving," Angie said as she stepped out of the car without looking back.

She slammed the car door and walked inside. Kayla had driven away after Derrick jumped in the front seat. She hadn't even put the car in park.

CHAPTER 12

Deena hadn't talked to her grandmother in almost three weeks. She picked up double shifts at the mall to make up the money it took to pay her aunt and uncle back for getting her car brought there. Since her grandmother went to bed super early every night and spent her entire weekends at church, there was no time for Deena to call her and check in.

She finally had the chance to talk to her one day.

"What's up old lady?" she joked. "Don't get on me because I haven't called you in a while."

"Yeah, so correct what you said. You're the busy one. Ran off south and I don't hear from you no more," her grandmother said sarcastically.

"I'm sorry grandma. I've been working double shifts to pay auntie and uncle back for helping me get my car here."

"How's it down there?"

"It's good. But I can't lie. I'm homesick."

"Yeah, you ain't never lived in the country. You're from the big city and young. It's hard for y'all to get used to livin' in such a small town like that. You should've stayed yourself right here. I don't know why you went running down there. It ain't nothin' there for you."

Deena wished she had kept it to herself that she was homesick but her grandmother would've known better.

"Yeah, I know grandma. But I'm doing good. I don't have any problems here. So, what's going on with you?"

Deena got off topic to avoid the lecture. She knew her grandmother wouldn't stop.

"I'm alright. Knees bothering me."

"Is Uncle Patrick still coming over to help you with stuff."

Patrick was Deena's uncle who drove her grandmother around sometimes to run errands.

"Yeah he's still comin. Tryin' to get me to sign up for those van rides to my appointments and stuff."

She took cabs to her doctor appointments, but her insurance didn't pay for rides anywhere else.

"What's the difference between the cabs and vans?" Deena asked.

"The cabs only take me to my appointments. Patrick found out the vans will take me anywhere for three dollars each way."

"Oh, that's not bad. You don't wanna do it?"

"Those vans usually have other people on 'em. And I don't wanna ride around while they take other people places too. I just wanna get where I'm going instead of being stuck on a van all day." She sounded frustrated.

"I only ever see like two people on those vans at a time. It's not a lot of people on 'em." Deena tried to convince her. "Grandma, it's better than waiting around for Uncle Patrick to do stuff for you. Sometimes he can't even come and take you places."

Deena thought it was a good idea for her. Her uncle Patrick didn't always help out and sometimes was a no show to pick her grandmother up. His mom was not always at the top of his priority list.

"Well, I told him I'll think about it."

She spoke fast as if to get Deena to leave it alone.

"That's a guaranteed ride and you won't be waiting that long to get picked up. And you can get rides to church on the weekend and get dropped off at the door," Deena pleaded.

"I said I'll think about it, Deena."

Deena knew that meant to move on.

"Okay. Anyway. I just called to check on you. I won't take so long next time. I gotta work a few more doubles coming up, but I'll call you on a break if I have to."

"I'm doing alright. Gettin' ready to sit down and look through my mail."

"I'll try to call you next week," Deena said.

They hung up.

She smiled to herself thinking of her grandmother. She missed her. She was ten years old when her mother died from pneumonia after being misdiagnosed by doctors. Her grandmother raised her and gave her the best childhood. Deena reminisced about her always telling her she was just like her mom. She saw how it still affected her over the years that she lost her only daughter who was her pride and joy. They were close and her grandmother kept a picture of her on her living room wall. Deena knew she wouldn't have to worry about her uncle helping out occasionally if her mom was still living. She would've made sure her grandmother was well cared for.

She suddenly felt guilt. Her grandmother had always taken care of herself but as the days went by, she was becoming more dependent on others, even though she had a hard time admitting it. There was no one to go to the doctor with her periodically like she did. Her lazy son sure wasn't going to do it. He could barely make time to take her for groceries. Deena would for sure go home in a heartbeat if she needed her.

She did miss home. She missed her job at Ward's. The money was decent too. Shawn managed to creep in her thoughts and she tried to dismiss him. Thinking of Ward's would always bring her work desk to mind and how she'd walk over and look out the window. Dooner Sausage sat across the street below, forever a part of the view. She had worked at Ward's for five years. How did thinking of it inevitably make her think of Shawn who she knew all of six months? He ruined her memories of that place. She wanted to only think of him and their time together, but it was hard. He wasn't there with her in the present like she wanted him to be. Their whole relationship was a lie. But how was it that she still smelled his scent and felt his lips against hers? She felt him inside her and his body on her. He was strong and soft at the same time. His lips between her legs grabbed and sucked, leaving his chin wet. She took a deep breath. It consumed her. She dreamt about it. Being away in a small, boring town didn't even help. He was constantly on her mind. She couldn't have him and it made her mad. She hated that she loved him.

She struggled over the next few days with the idea of going back home. She couldn't stand the thought of running into Shawn because she wasn't over him and what he did. That was still a work in progress and being away was proving not to work. She did miss the city and her favorite restaurants. She missed Angie and Tia and she especially missed her grandmother. She was the main reason she needed to return home. Starting completely over would sour the plan. She wanted to jump right back into the way things were. That meant getting her job back at Ward's. That also meant making sure a certain person wasn't still unloading trucks across the street there. She picked up the phone and called.

"Dooner Sausage can I help you?"

"Hi. Is there a way I could leave a message for stockperson Shawn Buchanan?"

She put on her best professional voice.

"Oh, I'm sorry ma'am. He no longer works here. Is there something I can help you with?"

"No. I was specifically looking for him," Deena said.

She thanked the receptionist and hung up. Her heart sank. Him saying he loved her played in her head like a song. It was hard not to think he left there because maybe it reminded him of her. Maybe looking across the street every day was hard for him too. Or maybe not. It didn't matter what he thought. She could make her next phone call. It was time to go home.

CHAPTER 13

Aaron Mantrell Little came into the world weighing six pounds and eight ounces. Angie always knew she had a boy inside her. She stared down at her little man and was a proud mom. He had come tiny, screaming with good lungs. She managed to call Brian when she went into labor so he could bring Tia to the hospital. Tia was all she had and he promised he'd get her there. They waited in the family area while Angie gave birth. Tia was happy to see her baby brother. She stared at him in Angie's arms and asked all the questions her seven-year old brain had stored. Brian came in and saw baby Aaron briefly. He congratulated Angie and left the room to give Tia time with them. Angie didn't feel right making him stay too long. He had a baby daughter due in a few more weeks and needed to be with his fiancé as much as he could outside of work.

"Go out there and get your dad," Angie said to Tia.

Tia came back into the room with him, his eyes bloodshot red. He had fallen asleep waiting. Angie thanked him and told him he could leave. She looked up at the ceiling and thanked God for giving Tia such a good dad. He never complained about anything when it came to his baby girl. She stared down at Aaron while he slept in her arms. She couldn't say the same for him. It was a relief that he only had Bruce's nose. The rest of him was all her. She hoped his looks would stay that way. She could stand to stare at herself all day instead of looking at a small version of the man who left her son behind. Someone tapped at the door and it slowly opened.

It was a nurse who walked Deena to the room. She had been back home a few weeks by then after getting her job back at Ward's. She was told she had to wait until August before being re-hired. The person who took her position was already being promoted and leaving. Deena gladly remained in Georgia for a few more months. She saved her money from her mall job to buy herself a plane ticket home and to pay for her car to be towed back. She made sure things ran smoothly for the most part. Angie worked her magic and got her landlord to hold an apartment for her. He even waived the security deposit. Deena was going to be right upstairs above her. She slept on her grandmother's couch for two weeks but that couldn't last long. She had to have her own space. It was who she was. Besides, her grandmother had a one-bedroom apartment. With all her collections and what-nots everywhere, it was crowded with a visitor, let alone someone actually staying there.

A blue *It's a Boy* balloon danced around above her head as she held the string. Angie had called her when she got to the hospital, but she couldn't make it in time to be with her. She had been on the other side of town and got stuck in traffic. Aaron was born so fast that Deena knew she wouldn't have made it even if there was no traffic at all. She put the balloon over by the window sill in Angie's room.

"This is all I can afford right now," Deena laughed.

"That's okay. Kayla's coming. I'm sure she'll bring the whole gift shop. I need to tell her to spend that money on some diapers.

"Let me see this little handsome man."

Deena carefully took Aaron from Angie's arms. She sat down and stared at him. His eyes stayed closed.

"Open your eyes so I can see who you look like," she spoke softly over him.

"He looks like me! Thank God for that," Angie said with relief.

"Well he has Bruce's nose that's for sure."

Deena noticed that right away. It was wide and Angie's nose had a long, thinner bridge. He was small and perfect with medium brown skin and soft black hair. He was in a peaceful sleep, brand new to the world.

Deena marveled over him.

"Aww he's so cute. I wish he'd open his eyes."

"Hey why'd the nurse bring you to the room? I gave you the room number. You forgot it?"

"Yeah I did. I forgot as soon as you told me. She

was the desk nurse. She said she thought she saw someone come in here. I guess she had to make sure your nurse wasn't all up in your hoo hah." Deena giggled. "Isn't that what they do when you have a baby? Constantly come back and forth checking you down there?"

Angie half giggled.

"Yes, they do and it's irritating."

Deena looked at her. Her eyelids were low.

"Have you had any sleep?"

"Only a little doze here and there."

"You heard from your mom?"

Deena knew this was a touchy subject for Angie.

"No, but I'm sure Kayla told my aunt and she'll let her know. I don't care one way or the other."

Angie didn't break her sleepy expression. She wasn't bothered by Deena bringing her up. She was over the whole mother-daughter relationship thing. The best thing she could do was make sure she was a good mother to her own kids and support them no matter what.

The nurse came in. Deena looked at Angie. She had fallen asleep. The nurse took latex gloves from the box on the wall and pulled them onto her hands. Angie's eye opened and she rolled them at the sight of her. Her vitals and hoo hah were good. Deena looked at her and smiled. It wasn't funny. Angie looked irritated when the nurse left. She asked Deena to brush her hair up in a ponytail but couldn't stay awake. Deena felt like she was talking to herself. She had heard giving birth was exhausting. Angie's hair was scattered across the pillow and Deena gathered it up, brushing all the edges.

"Now you don't look like such a mess."

Deena went over to the sink and washed her hands.

"I gotta pick this little man back up. I want him to open his eyes."

Aaron still slept——as newborn babies did.

"Thank you." Angie felt her hair. "This feels much better."

She looked at Deena one last time holding Aaron.

"He'll wake up soon. It'll be bottle time."

"Get some sleep before your nurse comes back digging around again."

"You got jokes," Angie said without laughing.

"No, I'm serious. Close your eyes. I'll stay with the baby for a while."

Deena held Aaron and it didn't take long for Angie to fall asleep. Her ponytail bun sat atop her head neat and unmovable. Even though the bed was raised leaving her in a sitting position, she slept not seeming to care. The room was quiet except for the TV. Deena turned it on and watched. She looked down at Aaron every now and then, still waiting to catch the brown shade of his eyes.

Apartment building living was not peaceful for a newborn baby. Doors slammed all the time. People came and went. Walls were paper thin. Even alarm clocks could be heard through the vents early in the morning. Angie lived on the first floor of their eight-unit building. Her door was only a few feet away from the front lobby door so she endured the most noise. Eight apartments meant someone always visited someone else. They talked in the hallways. Kids didn't walk. They ran. And people always rang the wrong doorbell—-especially hers. Quiet only came at night. Around midnight that was. Aaron got used to his new environment this way. The slammed doors startled him and the hallway noise in general woke him out of his sleep. Angie kept him in the bedroom with the doors closed when he napped. The boring nursery music CD she got as a baby shower gift helped. She got tired of opening her door asking the loud mouths to please keep it down so her baby could sleep.

Having Deena felt like a safety net. She wasn't alone. They visited each other of course. Listening to music and watching movies. It was mostly in Angie's apartment because all of Aaron's things were within reach. Her living room looked like a small day care center. His swing, play pen, and bouncy seat crowded what used to be open spaces around the furniture. Angie joked that the living room was Aaron's bedroom because he didn't have one. She couldn't think about a three-bedroom right now. She could barely afford the two she had. She hadn't thought about day care cost either. She managed to put that out of her mind since early in her pregnancy. It had become too much but now it was time. Kayla had told her about a program for single mothers that provided affordable day care. Aaron could start going in a few weeks. It still wasn't really "affordable" because she had to buy diapers and formula and since Tia was born, the prices had skyrocketed. Deena told her about giving Bruce's name to the child support agency. They'd track his social security number in case he had a job somewhere. Angie did it but didn't hold her breath on Bruce maturing all of a sudden, filling out applications.

CHAPTER 14

Deena rushed to her car leaving work to pick up her grandmother from an appointment. She had to pick up Angie first. They were going to Target for a sale. Deena agreed to drive her car so Angie could save her gas. She pulled up outside their building and Angie came out moving as fast as she could with Aaron in a car seat. He was almost three months old and weighed Angie's arm down. A big diaper bag hung over her shoulder. It weighed more than he did.

"We gonna make it to pick her up on time?"

Angie seemed out of breath putting her load in the car and getting Aaron's seat in. She didn't want to be responsible for making Deena's grandmother wait somewhere.

"We'll be a few minutes late but she can wait in the lobby. Hey lil man."

Deena looked in the back seat at Aaron who was wide-eyed, taking everything in. "Where's Tia?"

"With her dad. I gotta stop by there and get her on the way back. We're gonna watch a movie when Aaron takes a nap."

"How's she juggling a new baby brother and sister all at once?"

"That's why I'm giving her some one-on-one today."

Angie reached into the back seat and gave Aaron his pacifier back that had fallen into his lap.

"Oh, I take it the excitement wore off?"

"Well yeah. The babies are gettin' all the attention."

"Poor Tia," Deena said.

"So that's why today is her day but I feel bad that it's only a movie while he naps."

"Well one day while he's at day care and she doesn't have school, maybe you could take off work and give her a whole day," Deena suggested.

"Uh you forgot this is a broke chick," Angie said pointing to herself. "Taking off work is not an option."

Aaron spit out his pacifier again onto his lap. Angie reached over the seat to get it for him. She didn't notice he was fine without it and gently pushed it back into his mouth. Deena parked the car. She was ten minutes late and left Angie and Aaron to run inside and get her grandmother.

The waiting area was empty. She wasn't there. The receptionist told Deena that she ran into someone she knew and that person gave her a ride home.

"She told me to tell you," the receptionist said.

Deena looked puzzled--almost worried.

"She seemed excited to go with them. It was a married couple."

"Oohh-kay," Deena said, still looking confused. "I rushed to get here from across town."

She turned to leave. She headed for the door but was stopped in her tracks all of a sudden. It was *him*.

Shawn was walking in pushing an empty wheelchair. Their eyes locked. Deena felt like she stepped out of her own body for a second. Her feet made steps forward but she couldn't feel them. She had gone numb but snapped herself out of it and looked away from him. Shawn let go of the wheelchair and quickly walked toward her, cutting off her path to the door.

"Deena," he said stepping in front of her.

He stared at her.

"What?"

She looked away and focused her eyes on something across the room. She wanted to make her hands come up and push him out of her way, but she stood there. His scent hugged her and she couldn't move. It was the scent she fell in love with.

"I looked for you. Somebody at your job told me you quit and left town."

Shawn's voice was filled with guilt.

"You couldn't have come *too* soon. I was there for another month before I left."

Deena made eye contact with him for a second. She wanted to ask what took him so long.

"Listen," Shawn said calmly.

The wheelchair he had been pushing blocked people's way coming through the door. He didn't want to step away and move it over, afraid Deena would use it as her chance to bolt out the door.

"I didn't mean for all that to happen. I wanted to tell you my situation but I thought you would leave me. I was just trying to find the right time."

Deena tried not to look at him. Her eyes moved toward the floor and stopped at his left hand. He was wearing his wedding band—obviously still very married. He never wore it when they were together. A man wearing his ring meant he wanted it known he was off limits. He was still talking but Deena couldn't hear him. She kept her focus on the wall painting across the lobby.

The ring stunned her.

Here he was, standing right in front of her as a married man. She was even more furious, but she stayed calm. Shawn had been telling her how his wife had left for a while and moved away. He tried explaining his situation and told Deena that his marriage was on the rocks at that time. Deena heard some of it but tuned the rest out. She snapped out of her thoughts when Shawn stopped talking. She looked at him. They shared a brief awkward stare and he continued.

"I went by Ward's looking for you and they told me you left town," he repeated this trying to keep Deena in front of him as long as he could.

"I left because I was pregnant. I had a son."

Deena swallowed hard, not able to believe she actually said this. Pregnant? She knew she had never been pregnant. Why was she telling Shawn she had a son?

"What! By me?!"

Shawn's voice got louder. He looked as if his knees were going to buckle.

"Uh yeah. Who else?"

Deena was offended that Shawn would dare to ask her that. But she hadn't been pregnant. What son was she talking about? She suddenly wasn't like herself.

"When? Where is he?"

Shawn was stunned but managed to stay standing at what he was hearing.

"He's almost three months. I was embarrassed at being pregnant by a married man so I left."

Shawn hung on every word with his mouth a little open still in shock. Deena held her composure. She was straight-faced and serious. She could see she had him convinced. He knew she loved him when they were together. He loved her and had no reason not to trust that he'd made a baby with her.

"Where is he? Can I see him?"

Shawn seemed panicked and excited at the same time. The wheelchair he pushed in still sat in the way of people coming back and forth.

"He's in the car with Angie," Deena said.

Her heart raced fast. She was about to pass Aaron off as her own baby! She knew Shawn would ask to see him. He was asking questions faster than she could think. He took her response as an invitation to see who he thought was his son. At any moment she could let the wind out of his sails and tell him it was a lie. She was wrong if she thought she'd worry him about having a baby outside his marriage. He was clearly the opposite and seemed quite overjoyed minus the smile. His eyes said it too. Deena still had time to tell him the truth but she stood frozen.

He remembered he was at work and turned around nervously realizing the empty wheelchair was still there. He went to grab it trying to keep eye contact with Deena.

"Just let me return this wheelchair and I'll come right out," he said moving as fast as he could.

Deena didn't say anything. She turned to go out the door. She ran down the front steps of the building headed for her car parked in the circular driveway. She knew Shawn was probably just seconds behind her. Angie was reading a magazine in the front seat. She had her head down and didn't see Deena coming.

"Hey!"

Deena's hand clutched the top of the passenger window that was rolled half-way down. She had been running so fast that her body flung into the passenger door as she grabbed onto the window. She looked behind her and saw Shawn quickly walking down the front steps in her direction. There was no time to prep Angie for what was about to happen.

"I ran into Shawn. Here he comes. Just play along."

Deena moved away from Angie's view and stood at the back door of the car where Aaron was. He had fallen asleep. Angie saw Shawn headed toward them and gave Deena a quick okay without knowing to what she was playing along. Shawn slowed his pace as he got closer, almost bracing himself for the moment. He kept his eyes on the back window where Deena stood. She opened the door and Aaron still slept, his head leaning over on his car seat straps. Shawn bent his head down to look at him.

"Aww wow. He's so cute. And he kinda has my nose."

Angie swallowed and kept her face forward. She bulged her eyes knowing Shawn couldn't see her. She now knew Deena was passing Aaron off as her own son. How could she? And how was she going to pull this off?

She couldn't talk. She silently thanked God no one was saying anything to her. She listened to Shawn ask Deena an array of questions about Aaron, and Deena had a spur of the moment answer for all of them. His oohs and aahs over Aaron in the backseat gave Angie a sinking feeling in her stomach. He obviously bought whatever Deena sold him inside the medical building and was immediately attached to her son believing he had fathered him. She hung on every word between the two of them and suddenly had an uncontrollable cough when she heard what came next.

"Xavier Buchanan," Shawn said as he gently squeezed Aaron's leg with two of his fingers. "Oh, hi Angie. I'm sorry I didn't speak right away."

Shawn said this as if Angie's coughing snapped him back into reality.

"Hi," Angie said, beating herself in the chest. "You alright?"

Angie was overwhelmed with all of this on the spot. She kept her cool and tried to act normal in the moment.

"Yeah," Angie said, and got her cough under control.

Xavier Buchanan? Deena even came up with a different name for Aaron. Angie was convinced that Deena had lost her mind upon seeing Shawn. She couldn't have had this planned. Had she forgot all of a sudden that he's married?! With children?! Was wifey going to know about this?! Angie was beside herself, but she played like a robot and faced forward, immovable until it was over.

Deena gave Shawn her new phone number and agreed to let him see Aaron in a few days or so at her apartment. He walked away elated and she quickly got back into the driver seat. Aaron was still sleeping. Angie didn't let Deena put the car in gear before tearing into her.

"Girl, have you lost your mind?!"

"I'm so sorry. I saw him with that ring on and I just gotta pay him back for what he did."

Deena almost sounded like she was only talking to herself.

"I want revenge. That's all I gotta say."

"How do you think you can pull this off?"

"I will. Just work with me. We live in the same building. I promise I won't do it for long. I just wanna get him going good enough thinking Aaron is his son and then I'll tell him the truth. All of this stuff just came out of nowhere."

Deena explained that she never planned any of what happened and that it came to her in the spur of the moment as a revenge tactic. She told Angie it happened so fast and she wanted to make Shawn believe she really had a baby by him. She thought it would go over better with him thinking his son had his last name. Since she hadn't planned it, she winged it as she went. She reassured Angie that she'd drop the bomb on Shawn as soon as she had him in the right position.

Angie had to admit that she didn't like what Shawn did to her best friend, but at the same time, she felt sorry for him. She didn't say it out loud of course. She didn't know Deena felt that much rage over him not telling her he was married. This was taking revenge to another level.

CHAPTER 15

Shawn held onto Deena's word that he could see Aaron in a few days. He didn't hesitate to call and ask about a good time to come over. He made sure he cleared his work schedule. Nothing was more important to him than his kids. Deena could see that he would feel no different about Aaron than his own children. He had fallen hard for her bait and she knew the let-down would be detrimental. She told him to come at three o'clock. She went downstairs and got Aaron from Angie a half hour earlier. She grabbed his diaper bag and a few blankets. Aaron followed her around the room with his eyes after she laid him on the couch. She looked around the living room and made sure nothing was out of place.

Then it hit her.

None of his other things were there! How was he her baby and nothing was in her apartment that had anything to do with a baby? It was 2:45 and she knew Shawn was too excited to be even a second late ringing the bell. She left Aaron on the couch and raced down to Angie's apartment.

"I don't have any of his stuff! Shawn will be here in fifteen minutes!"

Deena panicked and ran in and grabbed one end of Aaron's baby swing.

"Help me get this upstairs fast."

"Where's Aaron?" Angie asked, taken by surprise.

"Upstairs on the couch. Come on hurry up."

Angie grabbed the other end of the swing and walked forward to the door while Deena backed out with it.

"Wait."

She stopped before backing over the door's threshold. She quickly peeked her head out of the lobby door window, making sure Shawn wasn't standing there ringing the bell.

"I'm making sure he didn't get here yet. We can't let him see us moving this."

Deena breathed hard, out of breath from running down the stairs, two at a time.

"Is this the only thing you're taking?"

"No. I'm gonna come back down to get the bouncy seat too. That should do it for now."

They lifted the swing and carried it up the stairs to Deena's apartment. Aaron had just started to cry after he followed Deena with his eyes and she hadn't come back into his view. Angie picked him up and softly patted his back. Deena positioned the swing in the living room and looked up at the clock over her TV. She went back down the stairs into Angie's apartment and grabbed the bouncy seat. Angie laid Aaron back on the couch and put his pacifier in his mouth. Deena made it back upstairs and the doorbell rang as soon as she sat the bouncy seat on the floor. Angie walked ahead of her down the stairs and slipped into her apartment. Deena opened the door and tried to keep a serious straight face. She had to resist putting her hand over her chest because her heart beat so fast, she thought he could see it. He followed her up the stairs and into the apartment.

"Thanks for letting me come by," Shawn said.

He walked over to the couch and sat down. Aaron was still sucking his pacifier. Shawn picked him up gently and softly talked to him.

"Hey little man. It's nice to see you again. It's daddy."

Shawn held him in one arm and looked down at him. Deena walked into the kitchen out of his view. She calmed herself down and went over in her head what she practiced about things he might ask.

"I can't believe I got another son."

He looked at Deena. She stood over by the kitchen watching him with Aaron.

"I can't say I'm sorry enough to you. I wish things could've worked out with us."

Deena stayed quiet and kept her serious look. She knew if he could read her mind, he'd put Aaron down and run for the door. She just stared back at him.

"I know you don't wanna talk about what happened with us, but if I hadn't saw you the other day, were you ever going to tell me I had a son?"

She paused for a moment, trying to think of her response.

"I would've eventually. I don't want my son growing up without his father."

That was a better answer than saying she wouldn't have. It probably would've led to a long conversation about the two of them and her anger toward what he did. Deena didn't want to drag his visit out with unnecessary talk. She wanted it to go as quick as possible. The faster it went with little said, the better. "Why did you name him Xavier?"

It was Shawn's middle name.

"I guess I like tradition when it comes to certain things. And since you already had a Shawn Jr, I gave Xavier your middle name."

Deena had this answer prepared. She rattled it off as if it was rehearsed.

"I mean don't get me wrong," Shawn caught himself, not wanting her to think it was a dumb question. "I'm happy for him to have my middle name. I just thought that from how I fucked up things with us, you would've never done that."

Deena stared at him thinking about the night she went to his house in a snowstorm.

"Damn baby. I can't say enough how sorry I am. You just don't know how I hated myself for that. I wish that would've turned out different."

He kept his eyes on her, still holding Aaron with one arm. She rolled her eyes and went over to her living room chair to sit down. Shawn apologized for bringing it up and changed the subject back to Aaron. He looked around the living room, noticing the swing and bouncy seat.

"You got everything you need for him?"

"Yeah," Deena said, keeping it short.

"You sure? He's got a bed and everything?"

"Yup. He's good."

Deena hoped he wouldn't ask to see Aaron's bed. She panicked a little. She wasn't going to attempt to move every single piece of baby furniture Angie had before he got there. She just had to keep him from seeing her spare bedroom to avoid that scenario.

"I mean it. Let me know if he needs anything. I don't expect you to do this all by yourself."

A half hour had passed. Deena had already told Shawn she only had about an hour for him to visit. She could smell his cologne and tried not to stare at his physique when he wasn't looking. She had to keep her mind on reeling him in to hurt him, not falling for him all over again. That would defeat the purpose. She got up and went into the bedroom as he was rocking Aaron on his lap.

"I'll be right back."

She closed the door and took a deep breath. She shook her head from side to side and rubbed her hands down her face. She loosened her shoulders and regrouped. She went back into the living room and Aaron had fallen asleep in Shawn's lap. They talked some more about setting up visits and compared their schedules. Deena made sure to keep it on her terms only.

"He's asleep. My hour is almost up anyway and I know you got things to do."

Shawn laid Aaron back on his blanket on the couch.

"I better go."

He stood up and reached into his pocket. He took some money out of his wallet.

"Here take this. I have to give you something. He's two months old and I know formula is expensive."

He walked toward Deena and she stood up and unlocked the door. He held the money out to her. She had to make this whole thing look good so she couldn't turn the money down. She took it and didn't say a word. She couldn't speak. Shawn smelled so good. She thought of how she'd put her face against his neck when they fell asleep after sex. His wedding band glared as he put his wallet back in his pocket. Deena opened the door and he stood in front of her, staring for a moment.

"Thanks again for letting me see him. I'll call you in a couple of days."

He put only a few inches in between them and stopped for a moment before going out the door. Deena didn't say anything. She closed the door behind him and rolled her eyes.

"Bastard. Wearing his ring over here. He's got some nerve," she said to herself.

She counted the money he gave her. It was fifty dollars.

"Well Angie can use this."

She called Angie's phone.

"Come up here. He left and Aaron fell asleep."

"How was it?" Angie asked as she stepped inside. She saw Aaron on the couch.

"It went alright."

"Did he fall asleep while Shawn was here?"

"Yeah he sat there rocking him on the couch."

"And he didn't cry from him holding him?"

Angie was surprised Aaron let Shawn hold him because he wasn't a familiar face.

"Nope. I thought he was gonna cry too." Deena was still upset. "You know that bastard had his ring on?"

Deena didn't give Angie a chance to ask what was wrong.

"Well I don't know what to say about that. I don't know what you expected."

Angie was confused as to why Deena was so upset over it. Was he supposed to now act like he wasn't married after she already knew the truth?

"Here." Deena handed her the money. "He gave me that for Aaron. You take it. It'll get him some diapers and stuff."

Angie laughed.

"I feel so guilty taking this. But I do need it."

She stuffed the money in her back pocket and walked over to the bouncy seat and picked it up.

"When is he coming back?"

"He said he'll call in a couple of days," Deena said. "I lied and told him Aaron starts daycare next week. He knows I've been working so I made him think one of my aunts has been keeping him for me."

"Well you won't be lying about daycare."

Angie headed toward the door with the bouncy seat, carrying it with one hand.

"Kayla is on her way to see Aaron and she said her friend's mother has a daycare. Aaron can go there for two hundred dollars a week. I guess I can't complain since other day care centers charge way more."

Angie could send him through the week but not on weekends. Deena kept this in mind, but planned to keep Shawn's visits on her own schedule.

———— ((●)) ————

For the next few weeks, Shawn came to visit Aaron at the apartment. Deena and Angie hauled baby stuff back and forth whenever he was coming. Deena even brought up Aaron's box of diapers and put them in the hall closet so Shawn could see them when he offered to change him. And Aaron was getting used to seeing him around. Shawn played with him and raised him in the air to make him smile. Deena moved around the apartment doing things or pretended to clean up. Sometimes she'd catch him staring at her. She had to remind herself that this whole routine was to get revenge. One day she stood at the kitchen table opening her mail. She looked and saw him staring again.

"Don't do that," she said.

"What?"

"Stare."

"I'm sorry. I can't help it. You know what we had. I can't forget about that."

Shawn looked back at Aaron and bounced him up and down on his leg.

"Yeah and I can't forget about how it was all a lie," Deena said rolling her eyes.

"No it wasn't. And look at what came out of it," Shawn said pointing at Aaron.

He pulled the bouncy seat closer to him on the floor and sat Aaron in it. He took out his cell phone and took pictures of him.

"What are you doing?!" Deena asked.

Shawn stopped and looked confused.

"What? I'm taking pictures of my son."

"Excuse me," she said.

She walked over and grabbed Aaron's bouncy seat and turned it around away from Shawn.

"You have a wife. I don't want her snooping through your phone and seeing him."

Deena knew she couldn't let anyone other than Shawn believe Aaron was his son. Even though she'd love to stick it to Shawn's wife too, it wasn't her fault Shawn stepped out on the marriage.

"She does not go through my phone first of all," Shawn said. "And second of all, he can't stay a secret forever. At some point I gotta tell her. I won't hide my son from anybody."

117

Shawn grabbed the edge of Aaron's bouncy seat and slowly turned it back around.

"Isn't that right Xavier?" He said as he leaned over looking at Aaron.

Aaron smiled. Deena would have to for sure end this before Shawn started telling people. She just had to think of when and how to do it. She slipped into her room and pretended to be busy. Shawn called her back into the living room after a few minutes.

"What's the name of the daycare he'll be going to?"

Deena was stumped. She hesitated. She never asked Angie the name of his daycare. Or where it was located.

"You know I actually don't know the name of it. My co-worker's kids go there."

Deena was embarrassed. She avoided eye contact with Shawn.

"I'm so stupid I never asked her the name of it," she laughed. "The name of it is really small on the door."

Shawn looked serious.

"Well where is it?" He asked.

Deena paused. She didn't know that either.

"81st and Washington."

She made it up. She had no idea if it was a daycare there or not, but she couldn't say she didn't know that either.

"Way out there?" Shawn asked.

"Yeah, it'll most likely be temporary because of

the distance. I just want him to go somewhere that somebody's familiar with."

She could leave the option open of "changing" the daycare once she talked to Angie. And she had a feeling Shawn didn't frequent 81st and Washington much so it was safe to call out on impulse. She was right.

"I just want to know where he's going to be when you're at work in case of an emergency."

Shawn stood up with Aaron as if he was about to leave. Deena was relieved hoping that was the case.

"Okay I'll let you know," she said.

It was all she could say. Shawn walked over and handed Aaron to her. It was time for him to go.

"I gotta go Xavier," he said to Aaron.

Deena took him and Shawn reached in his pocket getting his wallet.

"Here. Take this money. I haven't given you anything for him in the last few visits." He held out eighty dollars. "Oh, how much would daycare be?"

Deena knew this answer because she remembered Angie saying she could barely afford it.

"Two hundred dollars a week."

She kept her eyes on Aaron while she held him being sure not to look at Shawn.

"For real?!" He was stumped. "Man. I never had to put my kids in daycare, but I don't think it was that expensive back then."

"Yeah, that's a lot." Deena said, still not looking at him.

"We'll work something out the next time I come over."

Shawn headed out the door like he was in a hurry to get somewhere. Deena closed the door and sat on the couch with Aaron. She wanted to call Shawn's cell phone and tell him the truth right at that moment. She considered what might happen. Would he turn around and come right back acting like a crazy person? Would he curse her out and hang up? She saw how he was with Aaron when he visited. He started to form a bond with him and genuinely loved him. Even with only a month gone by, it would devastate him to find out the truth. Deena knew whenever she decided to tell him, it couldn't be face-to-face. She didn't know what his reaction would be.

She looked down at Aaron.

"I guess you probably want your mom now huh?"

She walked downstairs to Angie and handed her all of the eighty dollars from Shawn.

"I told him daycare is two hundred dollars a week. But he asked," Deena said.

"Ooh thank you," Angie said. "I could use every dime. I'm strugglin' here."

Angie spread the four twenty dollar bills out in her hand. It made her day. They said the usual "see you later," and Deena left.

She knew the money distracted Angie from asking how much longer the charade would be. She kept picturing how Shawn had become with Aaron. It made it harder for her to tell him he wasn't his son.

CHAPTER 16

The staff at My Babies Day Care greeted Aaron every morning when Angie dropped him off. The first couple of weeks new babies got "report cards" sent home with them. "*A very good baby*" was always on his. She saw his picture pinned to a huge bulletin board with the rest of the kids there. His curly head of hair filled the top of the four by six of him, and he definitely stood out from the rest. Aaron didn't cry when Angie left him. It felt good not to have the spoiled baby no one wanted to see coming. But it sometimes made her worry that he was becoming unattached to her. Besides daycare most of the week, he was with Deena. Shawn had paid up daycare for the full month. Angie finally had extra money in her pocket but she still pondered on whether to get a second job. One day Deena and Shawn would no longer be Aaron's fake parents and she needed to stay afloat on her own.

Mondays at the mall were never busy. The only people shopping during the day were mostly old, retired women. And they could care less about makeup. Angie figured whatever they owned as far as makeup was the Avon they all ordered from another elderly lady who sold it in her spare time. If they did happen to stop at her kiosk, they were looking for a gift for someone else. Angie did her regular shelf arranging and restocking the display cabinets at the kiosk. She put out the new sign that read: MAKE UP DONE FREE WITH A $30 PURCHASE. The week was going to be busy but she was excited about it. Doing makeup was her favorite thing, but she mostly just sold it at the kiosk. Someone usually only got their makeup done there maybe twice a week. Being free with a purchase meant people would at least try it. Even if it was just to get a new look for the day. The mall had just opened at 9AM and Angie wouldn't get busy for the next few hours. Her co-worker Samantha wasn't coming in until noon. She and Angie would switch back and forth doing makeup while the other worked the register for purchases. In the meantime, Angie sat at the register in one of the hardwood chairs and prepared for her butt to hurt all day. The hardwood was unforgiving on the derrière. She took the disinfectant spray from under the register and sprayed a paper towel to wipe the phone and register down.

"Hey Angie."

She looked up from wiping to see who was speaking to her. It was Brian's fiancé Tiffany. She was pushing their baby in a stroller. Angie had met her a couple of times when Brian dropped Tia back off at home.

"Hey what's up? What brings you to the mall this early."

It was 10:30.

"My aunt works at Nate's Appliances and she told me about a washer and dryer floor model that was half-off. We had to get up here early to buy it before it was gone."

She was alone pushing her baby, but she said *we.* Angie realized she came with Brian. She looked over the counter down to the stroller.

"Oh, that's cool. Look at you pretty girl," Angie said.

She focused on the baby right away. A little jealousy got in the way of her wanting to hold a conversation with Brian's fiancé.

"She's eight months old now, right?"

"Yeah," Tiffany said. "How's your son?"

"He's doing good. Getting big."

Brian came walking up quickly.

"Hey what's up girl?" He said smiling.

"What's up?" Angie said.

He came right up to the counter.

"How's the baby?"

"Good."

"I was gonna call you later today. Is he still in that same daycare you put him in?"

"Yeah."

Angie's forehead wrinkled at Brian asking about Aaron's daycare.

"I was gonna see if you could send Tia up there for some days after school."

He picked Tia up from school sometimes when

Angie had to work evenings. A new grocery store was opening and as manager, he was moved to that store to supervise second shift employees.

"I'll pay for it. It'll only be temporary," he said.

"Okay yeah I can sign her up. But you know it's forty dollars a day?"

He gave Angie a smirk.

"I got it," he said. "I'll see you later."

He turned to walk away. Tiffany pushed the stroller ahead and waved goodbye to Angie.

At least Aaron could be at daycare some days with his big sister. Angie couldn't complain. Especially since Brian was paying for it. Her situation was starting to get a little better by her picking up more hours at the kiosk. There were only three of them to man the kiosk, and they usually rotated days and hours leaving one person on a shift at a time. Thursday through Sunday always required two people. Those were the mall's busiest days.

One of the girls *only* worked during those days. She never wanted to work alone, either. She barely wanted to work at all. She still lived at home with her parents and didn't have to worry about bills so she gave a lot of her shifts to Angie. Angie saw the benefits of having more money. She also saw the downside of working so much. Aaron spent a lot of time at daycare besides being with Deena, and she only saw him later at night after nine o'clock. She already hadn't seen Tia as much, and now it was both her kids she wasn't able to spend time with. Shawn started coming twice a week to see Aaron, and it was sometime on Angie's off days. She'd be enjoying him crawling and starting to pull himself up onto things when Deena would come and whisk him away upstairs.

She certainly didn't want it to continue much longer. Aaron would be walking soon and even talking. Angie pictured him saying words and learning *mama.* She knew this was just as much her own fault as it was Deena's. She would rather have Aaron in daycare all day and night with her working more hours. She just couldn't handle him being confused about who was his mom. Her next conversation with Deena had to be a plan for bringing it to end.

Customers started filling the mall at the noon hour more so than earlier. A lot of people also sped through on their lunch breaks, including employees from the mall itself. Angie had a few customers just as her co-worker walked up and joined her. A woman criticized the "get your makeup done" offer with a purchase. Angie was in the middle of explaining to her that it was simply to help people get new ideas about color choices in eyeshadows, blushes, and lipsticks for their skin tones. Her tone was professional as always, but her brain was calling the lady a bitch. She felt people who were the most critical of something were usually the ones interested in it. She checked the lady out at the register and went back to straighten the display case when her phone rang.

"Hello," she said in a slight whisper.

It wasn't good to be seen on her personal phone with potential customers walking up.

"Hey what's up?"

It was Kayla. She whispered back, kidding around with Angie. She walked up and was at the makeup stand.

"Oh, hey," Angie said not smiling.

She hung up her phone and put it away. Kayla had to want something. She was not the mall going type. She always settled for a T.J. Maxx or Kohl's where she could find a good deal and do her shopping all at one store.

"I haven't asked you for a while," she said with her eyes slightly bulging and a smirk to her lips. "But I need the car."

Angie rolled her eyes.

"How'd you get up here? And why didn't you call first?" She stopped abruptly. "Wait a minute. Didn't you just get a new car?!" Her eyebrows curled inward.

"Yeah, but Derrick is going out of town in it for a couple of days. He dropped me off."

"No, you cannot have my car for a *whole couple of days*."

Angie tried to keep her voice low. A customer walked up and was looking at the lipstick testers, rubbing them on the back of her hand.

"Well, I got it all straightened out with work. Somebody took my shift for the next two days and I took theirs for the weekend," Kayla said it as if she knew Angie would agree. "I can drop you off at work and whatever else you need me to do."

The lady stood there waiting to be acknowledged after testing the lipsticks.

"We'll talk about it later, but I don't know about two days Kayla. That's a lot. I got kids in daycare you know? They need to be picked up too."

Angie reached under the register in a drawer and got out her purse. She pushed it to Kayla on the counter.

"Get my keys out of there. I'm parked by Macy's where the men's section is."

Angie rolled her eyes again and turned around to the other counter.

"Yes ma'am. How can I help you?" She asked with a fake smile.

Kayla hurried out of the mall swinging Angie's car keys in her hand.

CHAPTER 17

Deena got home from work and tossed her purse on the couch. She worked two extra hours to help with one of the store's inventory and she was wiped out. A laundry basket of clothes sat on the floor where she left it. She picked it up and took it into her bedroom. It was out of sight and out of mind for the moment. She had no energy to fold and put away clothes. She turned on the TV and kicked off her shoes. As soon as she fell back on the couch, the doorbell rang.

"Somebody's gotta have the wrong apartment," she said out loud.

She wiggled her feet back into her shoes at the door and walked downstairs. She would just tell whoever it was that they rang the wrong bell and go back upstairs. She looked through the side glass window panels next to the lobby door. It was Shawn. They hadn't set up the day for him to see Aaron. What was he doing there? He had never just come by unannounced and she didn't have Aaron. He was with Angie or probably still at daycare. Angie wasn't home either. Deena knew she couldn't ignore Shawn and pretend she didn't see him. He saw her look out the side window. Everything flashed before her. Aaron wasn't there. His stuff wasn't there. How would she explain all that? She was supposed to break it to Shawn in her own way, not have him catch her in the act! She had to wing it again to come up with something. She was becoming a pro at it anyway.

She opened the door, but stood there so Shawn got the hint that he couldn't come in. She gave him a serious look and let her face do the talking.

"Hey. I know we didn't set up a visit today," he talked fast seeing the look on Deena's face. "I just gotta talk to you about something. It couldn't wait."

"You couldn't call first?"

Deena crossed her arms and stayed in the doorway.

"My phone fell in the toilet last night and got messed up. I'm without a phone until tomorrow."

"Well Xavier is not here."

Deena was thinking fast about what to say. Whatever Shawn had to talk about wasn't as important as her figuring out what to say about where Aaron was.

"He's still at daycare? I thought you pick him up on your way home from work?"

"He's with my aunt. She wanted to keep him for a couple of days."

"Oh." Shawn looked confused but quickly got back on topic. "But I really have to tell you something."

"I'm listening."

Deena didn't move.

"Well, do we gotta have everybody in our business?"

Shawn held his arms out pointing out the obvious to her that they were standing in the front door of the apartment building. Deena rolled her eyes and turned around to walk upstairs. What the hell did he have to tell her? She was the one keeping a secret. Not the other way around. She walked in the apartment and turned to face him. She folded her arms across her chest and he saw she was unhappy with his popping by.

"I can see your *real* happy to see me," he said sarcastically.

Deena stayed still and didn't speak waiting for him to say what he had to say.

"I told my wife about Xavier," Shawn said.

Deena immediately felt sick and unfolded her arms.

"Huh?"

She could hardly speak but managed to breathe it out.

"Well, I told my mother first," Shawn went on. "And she convinced me to tell my wife."

"Oh my God. You did not do that."

Deena felt herself unraveling. She sat down to keep her feet from giving out underneath her. This was spiraling out of control. His mom *and* wife?! Two more people knew about Aaron.

That wasn't supposed to happen.

"I couldn't keep it from my mom anymore. I wanted to tell her so bad about how I messed up, but that she had a new grandson," Shawn went on explaining. "She wasn't happy of course about how it all came about, but she was excited about having a new grandson."

Deena fanned herself. She wanted to tell Shawn to shut up so she could think.

"But I told my mom about how my wife left and I met you and fell so hard for you. And I love Xavier to death. I don't care how he was conceived. He's my son and I just couldn't keep him a secret anymore."

Love him to death? Deena was even more afraid to tell Shawn the truth. He had truly fallen in love with Aaron being his son. She couldn't devastate him. Especially in that moment, there'd be no telling how he'd react. If she wasn't going to tell him, she couldn't seem so overwhelmed. She stared at the floor still sitting on the edge of the couch.

"So, what did your wife say?"

It got quiet. Shawn finally didn't speak for a second. It was obviously something he didn't want to think about.

"She slapped me a few times," he said uncomfortably. "And threw my phone in the toilet. So that's what actually happened to it. I just couldn't say that at the door."

"So now what?"

Deena kept her daydream stare, still in shock.

"Well, I don't wanna talk about her. I came to tell you that they know now, and more importantly my mother knows. I wanna be able to do stuff with my son and take him places. I want him to meet his brother and sister and I came to tell you that I don't want him to be a secret. I can't do this sneaking over here to see him and being his father sitting on the couch for an hour at a time."

Shawn stopped to see Deena's response.

She couldn't speak. She wallowed in the mistake she made. It would kill him to know Aaron wasn't his son. And he even told his mother. So, two people would be crushed by the truth, not just one.

Didn't mothers usually second-guess this kind of stuff and encourage their sons to get paternity tests? Surely, if they thought their sons had a fling outside of marriage. Deena thought about all of this, maintaining her stare at nothing. She knew Shawn would never question the paternity of Aaron because he truly believed he was his son. It wouldn't work anyway if he did. The two of them would have to be present for DNA testing and it would show that she wasn't even Aaron's real mother. That was even worse.

"Why aren't you saying anything?" Shawn was confused about Deena's cold silence. "I hope you don't have a problem with me wanting more time with him?"

"Huh?"

Deena seemed as if she had been shaken out of a deep sleep.

"N..no," she said.

She went to her go-to phony excuse to fit the situation every time.

"I'm just embarrassed about having a child with a married man. I told you that."

"What's this got to do with you? He'll be with me. My family knows nothing about you."

Shawn was still confused by it. He pleaded with her to see things his way.

"Look. I hate what happened to us," he said.

He walked around the coffee table and sat next to her on the couch.

"I fell hard for you and wasn't honest about my situation."

He grabbed her hands and turned her toward him.

"This sounds crazy but I'm glad we made a baby together. Even though we're not together, I'll always feel the same way about you."

His voice softened. Deena looked at him and then looked away. He gently turned her face back toward him and kissed her. He didn't separate his lips from hers and she kissed back. He grabbed her face and kissed harder, pulling her toward him. He pulled up her shirt running his hands over her breasts with his lips still locked to hers. He snatched at her bra, desperate to get it off. She grabbed at the buttons on his shirt and quickly undid each one until she was able to force it off his shoulders. They attacked each other, relieving the sexual tension between them. Deena lost herself in him and remembered how good he felt inside her. She forgot about everything with him pushing up and down against her. They didn't talk. They only breathed heavy with the TV noise in the background and the couch bumping against the floor. She moaned as Shawn came inside her. He couldn't pull out. She didn't want him to.

"I'm sorry," he said in her ear. "You felt so good. I couldn't get out."

"I didn't want you to, but that's not a good thing."

"Don't worry. I'm fixed. I still should've asked first though."

"Fixed? When did you get fixed?" Deena asked.

"A couple of months ago," he said.

"Just a couple of months ago?"

He believed Aaron was his son then.

"What made you do that all of a sudden?" She asked.

Shawn had slid his body down to put his face against her neck.

"I got three kids now. That's enough for me," he said.

"Does she know you got fixed?"

Deena tried not to sound shocked. If his wife didn't know about Aaron until now, did she know he went and got himself snipped?

"Huh?" Shawn started to raise up off her. "Well, that's part of the reason I haven't been home in two days. We had talked about having another baby before she decided to up and leave. She brought it up again a few months ago and I told her I didn't wanna do it. I told her I'm good with us having two kids and then I made an appointment to get the procedure done."

Shawn stood up and put his pants back on.

"So, I told her I made the appointment. That was that. But really, I did it because I didn't want any slip-ups. I have three kids already and I don't want anymore."

"Oh my God," Deena interrupted. "You told her no to a third baby and she finds out you already have a third baby with me?"

Deena's thoughts seeped out of her mouth. She was losing her calm out loud.

"And now she can't have another baby because you got fixed?"

She sat up and picked up her pants from the floor. She put them on in a hurry with her eyes unusually widened.

"Yeah." Shawn watched her move so quick all of a sudden. "Why is that making you freak out?"

"This is a messed up situation," Deena said.

She knew it couldn't get any worse. Shawn had actually wanted a third child, but now he could never have one after thinking he truly fathered one already! The lunch she ate at work almost came up from her stomach. She swallowed hard to keep it down.

"Don't worry about it."

Shawn reasoned with her. He didn't know what was happening inside her. That she almost hurled vomit his way.

"Just know that I'm gonna take care of my son. Don't worry about my situation."

Deena couldn't hear him for picturing him with a choke hold around her neck until she turned blue and was lifeless. She knew Shawn wasn't a violent person, but something like this would for sure turn him into a murderer. It would at least bring him close to it.

"Hey." He spoke louder to get Deena's attention.

She drifted off into her thoughts and seemed to tune him out.

"I wanna come and get Xavier tomorrow and take him to see my mom."

Shawn picked up his car keys he'd sat on the coffee table. He reached down and took both of Deena's hands and pulled her to her feet.

"Will he be back from your aunt's house?"

"Huh?" Deena hadn't heard him.

"I said my mom wants to see Xavier. Is he gonna be back from your aunt's house tomorrow?"

"Um, no." She needed time to think. "He'll be with her one more day."

Shawn grabbed her hands again and held them.

"I meant what I said about how I feel about you. And I'm not trying to complicate things. I just wanted to be with you again like before and I couldn't contain myself this time."

She stared up at him and hung on every word.

"If you don't want that to happen again, I understand," he said.

Deena let go of his hands and stepped back from him. Mom, wife, sex, and being fixed was all too much for her.

"I don't know what I want to happen right now Shawn," she said. "I can't think."

"Okay. I'm sorry again for springing all this on you and I'll keep my hands to myself next time."

Shawn walked to the door. He turned around and looked past Deena across the living room.

"Where's Xavier's swing and stuff? You always keep it in here."

"I sent it with him over my aunt's house so he could have it."

Shawn looked over to the kitchen.

"His highchair too?"

"Yep," Deena said quick.

Shawn's eyebrows turned down and his forehead wrinkled, showing he was confused.

"Ohhh-kay," he said. "I'll see you in a couple days."

He turned and walked out the door.

CHAPTER 18

Angie didn't take Deena's latest news about Aaron so well. Deena knew she wouldn't. She appreciated all the help that came along with the whole thing, but she was ready for it to be over. That couldn't happen for a while and she didn't want to think about how long it would actually take. Deena had begged her to let them keep it going because she was afraid for her life if Shawn found out. Angie certainly didn't want to be the reason her friend ended up hurt because she kept her son from the charade. But she also didn't want her son going off with a complete stranger to God knows where.

"Look, I trust him. He'll take good care of him." Deena tried to reassure her.

"I don't know him. You do. And neither of us know anything about his mother or who's at her house."

"Well, he told me it's just him and his mom since he's been staying back with her temporarily," Deena said.

Angie blew out a big breath.

"Deena, I didn't want another baby right now. That's not a secret. But now that he's here, I wouldn't have it any other way. Just because I'm getting help with taking care of him, doesn't mean I'm okay with not having him around. I really don't see him as much as I should because of working extra days now. And then on the days I can spend time with him, I gotta send him upstairs to you."

Deena felt bad. She knew she should've told Shawn a lot sooner and now it was too late. She didn't dare tell Angie she slept with him. Angie would for sure take Aaron and run thinking she'd only want to keep this going to have Shawn back in her bed. Angie walked into the bedroom and came back with Aaron's diaper bag. She dropped it on the couch and fumbled through a laundry basket of clothes on the living room floor. She put a pair of Aaron's pants and a shirt in the bag. She moved around the apartment not talking anymore. Deena stayed quiet too so not to make matters worse. She let Angie have her moment to be upset.

"I'm only putting a change of clothes in his bag out of habit. It doesn't mean he's staying overnight."

Angie didn't look at Deena. She grabbed Aaron's can of formula and put it down in the bag.

"He's not keeping him overnight," Deena spoke up. "I already told him he's been at my aunt's house the last two days."

Angie sat the diaper bag over by her. She had been sitting on the edge of the couch.

"Thank you," Deena said.

She picked up the bag and grabbed Aaron's car seat that always sat near the door.

"I'll come back and get him after I take this upstairs."

Aaron was asleep on Angie's bed. She made Deena go in and get him when she came back. Deena picked him up from the bed waking him out of his sleep, and went back upstairs to her apartment. Shawn was coming at three o'clock. She laid Aaron down on the couch and gave him his pacifier. He was starting to fall back off to sleep. Deena walked over to his diaper bag. His tiny jacket was sticking up out of the top of it and she needed to put it on him when Shawn got there. She stopped when she bent down to grab it out. *AARON L* was written in all caps on the side of the bag! Her heart beat fast.

Shawn couldn't see that. She went over to the car seat and looked all around the front of it. She turned it over and saw it written on the bottom. It was permanent marker of course. Deena panicked and Shawn was coming in another fifteen minutes. She tore through Aaron's diaper bag as fast as she could. The can of formula and his jacket were the only two other things someone used a black sharpie on to write his name. She ran to the window to make sure Shawn wasn't pulling up out front.

She came up with a quick fix.

She grabbed Aaron from the couch and jolted him out of his doze. She ran back downstairs with him and knocked on Angie's door.

"You gotta take him back right now!" She pushed him forward right into Angie and she grabbed hold of him. "I gotta go buy him a new diaper bag and some formula!

Deena was panicked.

"Why?" Angie looked confused.

"His stuff has his name all on it! I can't let Shawn see that when he thinks his name is Xavier. Did you write that on all of his stuff?"

"No. The daycare staff did that so they don't mix up the kids' things."

"Does he have another jacket here that they didn't write on?" Deena spoke quick and looked out the window to make sure Shawn wasn't coming.

"No. His coat has it too," Angie said.

"I'll be right back. Give me about thirty minutes."

Deena ran through the building to the back door and out to her car in the lot. She sped away. Angie closed the door and sat down on the couch with Aaron. She held him out in front of her and looked at him.

"She lost her mind, didn't she?"

Aaron just stared back and sucked his pacifier. He was always a good sport.

Deena called Shawn and told him she wouldn't be home for another hour. Luckily for her he said he was running behind anyway. She made it to the nearest Target five miles away and rushed in on her mission. She threw a diaper bag in the cart and pushed on to the formula and baby food aisle. It was a good thing Aaron was in his last days of getting formula. A twenty-two-ounce container was twenty dollars. She passed the car seats and strollers on her way to the baby clothes to get a jacket. She stopped quick and remembered Aaron's car seat with his name on the underside. After seeing $79.99 on the price tag for what looked like the cheapest one, she knew she had to take her chances with the car seat. Shawn couldn't have a reason for looking underneath it. She didn't have that kind of money anyway. Having to suddenly buy baby stuff let her see what Angie was going through. She paid for her things and raced home with a half hour to spare. She grabbed the diaper bag and went to Angie's apartment.

"I'll change this out here."

Deena had her hands full when Angie opened the door. Aaron was standing at the coffee table holding on.

"Look. He can stand and hold onto the table now. I started letting him do it couple days ago."

Angie ignored Deena's panic. She was proud of Aaron.

"Oh. I didn't know he could do that yet," Deena said.

She quickly tore the tags off the bag and jacket and she packed it with the things from the other bag. She went over to Aaron and picked him up.

"Sorry baby. We gotta head back upstairs and get your new jacket on so you can go bye-bye," she said in a baby voice to him.

Angie looked out the window and saw Shawn coming up the front walk to the door.

"Your ex or whatever you call him is coming to the door," she said.

"Oh shoot! I gotta run upstairs so he won't see me in the hallway!"

Deena grabbed up Aaron and the diaper bag. She had only gotten one arm inside his jacket. She ran up to her apartment and dropped the diaper bag on the floor when the doorbell rang. She made it just in time. She turned back out the door holding Aaron with one arm still out of his jacket. She tried to slow down to catch her breath. She let Shawn in and walked back up to the apartment.

"I was just putting his jacket on."

"Okay. I'll have him back by eight," Shawn said smiling at Aaron. "My mother can't wait to see him. Don't be surprised if he comes back with a ton of stuff. She is the queen of spoiling."

Shawn belted Aaron down in the car seat and Deena handed him the diaper bag. He swung it over his shoulder and picked up Aaron in the car seat with no effort. He hadn't noticed the crisp new look of the bag and as long as he didn't turn the car seat over, Deena was in the clear.

CHAPTER 19

Aaron learned to walk over the next few weeks just before his first birthday. Angie bought a small cake and ice cream to celebrate with just him and Tia. Tia had already noticed he wasn't home sometimes and she was smart enough to know it wasn't daycare days. Angie told her Deena liked keeping him and that Deena was helping her pay for diapers and stuff. She told her that Aaron's dad wasn't around like hers, and she appreciated Deena's help. As long as Tia didn't know Deena was really pretending to be Aaron's mom, Angie was okay with that excuse.

It was good that as a one-year old, Aaron didn't really understand birthdays and parties. Deena had given him a birth date two weeks after his real one, and of course Shawn had something planned for him. He told his kids about Aaron but they had yet to meet him.

Angie wished Aaron could tell her how much fun he had at his "second" birthday party. Shawn had sent pictures of him to Deena's phone. They were at some type of bounce house place. "HAPPY FIRST BIRTHDAY XAVIER" was on a small sheet cake and Aaron stood on a chair in front of it. A kid's hands held him up on the chair for the picture. It had to be one of Shawn's kids. Angie figured Shawn took the three of them to celebrate but he only sent pictures of Aaron. He brought Aaron back that evening with new stuff. He made two trips from the car hauling a big Baby Gap bag and both arms were full of toys. His mother bought most of it.

Shawn laughed telling Deena she was in for it. He was right about his mother being in the business of spoiling her grandkids. Deena couldn't wait to get it all out of her living room when he left. The neat freak in her couldn't allow things to fill up too much space. She transferred it right to Angie's apartment that was already crowded with Aaron's things. Angie was happy Aaron had a great "second birthday," but not happy to see her apartment get hoarded with big bulky toys. There was no more room for them.

Aaron walked to a box with a noisy push toy.

"We gotta haul all this up and down the stairs too? I'm sure Shawn will expect to see these toys when he comes to visit."

"I didn't think of that."

Deena stared at it all.

"You need to take some of this right back to your apartment. He can play with it when he's up there with you."

Aaron banged the toy as hard as he could.

"See? He can drive *you* crazy with some of this," Angie said.

Deena picked up what she could carry in two

hands and walked back up to her apartment. She didn't say a word. Angie was right. Shawn would ask where the stuff was he and his mom bought. She went back and got a couple of more things. She walked out not looking back.

"I'm tired. I'll talk to you tomorrow probably."

"Okay," Angie said.

Deena left and went back to toy land in her living room. She rolled her eyes and plopped down on her couch. Her situation had grown legs and was bigger than she was. She grabbed the remote control and channel surfed. She stopped on the FX channel showing the movie *Life* with Eddie Murphy. He was in the middle of reading a letter to a fellow prisoner who couldn't read. Deena laughed. The movie was still funny no matter how many times she'd seen it. She held the remote to change channels in between commercials, but dozed off to sleep.

She had it.

She thought of telling Shawn she slept with someone else before the relationship ended and Aaron wasn't his son. She called him and broke the news. He had questions. And more questions.

"How can that be? You told me he was my son."

Shawn was obviously upset and confused.

"I know. But I knew it was good chance he may not be."

"Look, I know I messed up and wasn't honest with you, but you can't deny that I love you. You said you felt the same way."

"I know. I did." Deena faked her reaction. "It was a one-time thing with somebody."

"I have loved Xavier since I laid eyes on him. I told my wife and mother about him! I got a vasectomy after him! He had better be my son!"

"I know. I'm sorry and I truly feel bad."

"I'm too attached to him now. I want a DNA test. If he's not my son I'll move on. But I don't believe he's somebody else's. I'll get it started myself."

Shawn walked out and slammed the door behind him. Deena popped her eyes open. The remote control fell to the floor. All she could hear was Martin Lawrence yelling at the prison baseball game on *Life*. She realized she dozed off. What she thought was a good idea in a dream wasn't one at all. She thanked God she hadn't done that already. There was no way Shawn could file for a DNA test. There was no record of her giving birth to a baby at all, let alone one named Xavier. It would show that she wasn't the mother and all hell would break loose. The only thing to do was make sure he never found out the truth.

She let out an ironically loud laugh at the movie. The jail warden held up his brown skinned grandson in front of all the inmates asking, "Who is the pappy?"

CHAPTER 20

Deena made sure to stay connected with her grandmother as much as she could in the midst of her mess. She agreed to travel south with her to visit her siblings she hadn't seen in years. Her sister was ninety years old and sick, being cared for by an in-home caregiver. Her brother was in the next town over but refused to travel out of state. She got cleared by her doctor to go as long as she wasn't alone. Deena was able to get two weeks off from work to take her. She went to check in on her a few days before the trip to make sure she wasn't packing the whole apartment to take with her. And it was just as she thought, but her grandmother had more things lying around with tags on them than her own clothes.

"What's all this grandma?"

"These are some gowns I'm taking to my sister and I got her some new sheets and stuff for her bed."

She pointed at things she had sat on the couch to pack. Deena noticed six or seven mason jars filled with an unappealing brown mixture.

"What's this? And why you got so many of em?"

"Apple preserves Rosalee made for me to take."

Rosalee was her friend and neighbor from the building.

"Grandma, you tryin' to take all that too?! Who are you giving that stuff to?" Deena was shocked.

"I'm taking it to give to them. I asked Rosalee to make it because I can't make all that stuff anymore. I can't stand up in the kitchen and cut all that fruit and stuff."

"Grandma your sister is niney and bedridden. What is she gonna do with some preserves?"

Deena couldn't believe she was planning on taking so much extra stuff. Her grandmother was not up for being questioned or talked out of doing something. She set Deena straight right away.

"Young lady I do have more than a sister down there. My brother and his wife are there and I got a couple of cousins and some nieces and nephews there. I haven't been down there in ten years so don't tell me what to take and what not to take. How you know they don't have gifts for me when I get there?"

She turned around and kept arranging things.

"Okay. I'm staying out of it. Say no more."

Deena knew to let it go. She didn't want to irritate her grandmother. She'd wait for the small rental car to get overloaded and then say she told her so.

She gave Deena the key to her storage in the basement for her to get a box to put the jars in for the trip. Boxes and bags were piled to the ceiling in the tall narrow storage. Deena spotted a box she thought she could move without making them all crash down on her head. She pushed her hand against one and wiggled it out from underneath the rest. Her cell phone rang in her top shirt pocket. It was Shawn. She ignored it and put the phone back. He left a message on her voicemail. She finished getting the box down and went back to the apartment. She'd wait until she left her grandmother to check his message and call him back. She told him about her trip and being gone for two weeks. She made him think Aaron was staying with her aunt until she came back.

She struggled up the stairs with the box. It was heavy with whatnots or something. There was no use emptying it in the storage first because it had no space left. Deena sat the box at the door and pushed it with her feet to get inside. She was out of breath.

"What's in here?"

She gave her grandmother a confused look.

"I don't know. Some of that stuff's been down there since I moved here. Open it and see."

"Man, this was heavy. You think this is a big enough box for your jars of apple stuff?"

Deena opened it and saw things wrapped in newspaper.

"Yeah, they'll fit in there," her grandmother said.

Little ceramic whatnots were in separate pieces of newspaper on top of more wrapped large pieces of heavy pottery. Deena kept them in the paper and carefully placed them on the table.

"I got some big brown paper bags for those jars.

Just tear 'em and wrap the jars with that," her grandmother said.

Deena saw that she dragged a huge plastic bag of clothes from her bedroom closet and was taking some out of it. She went over to the kitchen and tore the paper bags into pieces. She wrapped the jars of preserves in them and placed them in the box. She rolled her eyes. The box was too big for the jars and a big space was left on one side. She could've pulled out a smaller box in the storage had she known. She tore some more of the paper bags and stuffed the extra space with them to fill the box tighter for the trip.

She wondered about the clothes her grandmother was pulling out. She had a pile of them on her knee as she roused through the bag.

"What you gonna do with those clothes?"

"I'm taking some of this to my cousin Liz. I don't wear a lot of this no more and I know she'll be glad to get it."

Deena wondered why she had to take *everybody* something.

"Okay. I'm outta here. I'm going to reserve the rental car. Don't forget it's a small car grandma."

"I'm not taking too much Deena. But I am taking my small cooler because my brother said he'll take me to get some country sausage while I'm down there."

She never looked up from the bag of clothes.

"Okay," Deena said, rolling her eyes.

She closed the door and let out a huge loud sigh.

CHAPTER 21

The last time Angie heard anything about a wedding was when Deena talked about her cousin Toni's wedding. The ugly green dresses were what stuck out the most. Now she had been asked to be a part of one and she was in the best mood ever. Her services had been requested to do the makeup. She didn't have to be one of the girls stuffed into a poofy, big bow dress. She just had to make them look good in whatever they wore. Kayla was in the wedding and the bride was her friend. She told her Angie could do the girls' makeup for much less than other prices she had been given. And even better, it was that she could do it at the wedding venue. She just had to figure out how to handle Aaron and do makeup for eight girls at the same time. Deena was taking her grandmother out of town and made Shawn believe Aaron was staying with her aunt. Angie would've welcomed Deena's charade for once and let him go with Shawn for the day. Aaron was walking and curious about everything. He was at the typical age of touching things and knocking them over not to mention putting things in his mouth. Angie couldn't take her eyes off him. He once picked up a tube of lipstick from her makeup kit and bit off the tip. Luckily it wasn't a good taste in his mouth and he spit it out. She had been on the phone with her back to him for just a few seconds and he had a mouth full of red lipstick. Her only other option for the wedding was daycare, but the owner was on a trip also and gave her staff off that weekend. At least Kayla was a bridesmaid. Angie planned to make her help with Aaron and agree to getting her makeup done last.

It was three weeks from Christmas. Kayla's friend loved Christmas time and set her wedding date close to it. Sleek red strapless dresses with green bouquets, was her choice for the bridesmaids. Toni's idea of hunter green dresses would've worked for this wedding. Angie packed her makeup duffel bag and dressed Aaron to head for the church. She got an invite to stay and see the wedding so she dressed him and herself appropriately. She packed him some toys in his diaper bag and hoped Kayla could keep him under control.

Eight bridesmaids filled the ladies lounge at the church. Their purses and clothes were displaced all around the room. Some girls were still working on their hairstyles, pinning their updos just like the bride wanted. Angie struggled to move around the room squeezing by people trying not to step on stuff strewn on the floor. She had her duffel bag over her shoulder with Aaron in both arms hanging awkwardly. She found a space on one of the couches and plopped him down.

"There's my little man."

Kayla saw them from the other side of the room. She stepped around things on the floor to get over to them.

"Hey. Watch him while I run back to the car to get his bag," Angie spoke quietly.

Kayla was the only person she knew. She ran out to her car and saw two of the groomsmen arriving with tuxedos over their shoulders. Angie got back inside with the diaper bag. She pulled out his small toys quick to keep him from zoning in on one of the purses on the floor. She pulled up a chair and got started on the first bridesmaid. The bride had given strict instructions to use soft reds where she could on each girl. She was definitely sticking to her Christmas theme.

Angie worked straight through without a break and was on the fifth bridesmaid. Kayla managed to keep Aaron occupied and out of the way in the crowded room. Angie's phone rang in the pocket of her duffel bag. She stopped to see who was calling and stuffed it back down in the bag. It was Deena. She'd call her back when she was done. She thought she just wanted to talk about the trip or something. Deena left a voicemail message and Angie could hear the indicator beep. She selected an eyeshadow from the kit and carefully brushed it across the girl's eyelids. Her phone rang again. Deena was calling back.

She was still driving on the trip but pulled over to a rest stop so she and her grandmother could use the bathroom. Shawn called her. She had forgot to check his voicemail message from the day before when she was in her grandmother's basement. His family Christmas pictures were being taken that afternoon at his mother's church and he told Deena two weeks before that he wanted Aaron to be in them. Every five years his mother wanted new family pictures around Christmas time. Deena forgot about it and had told him Aaron was staying with her aunt while she was gone.

"Okay well I need to get him just for these pictures and I'll take him right back. I told you about this. This is the only day the photographer can be at the church," he said.

"But that's the problem. He's not with my aunt today. He's with Angie at some girl's wedding."

Deena hoped by saying this he'd let up on getting Aaron.

"Okay can you call her and tell her I can come get him? Wait. Why is he with Angie and at a wedding of all places?"

"She's doing makeup for the bridesmaids. My aunt had something to do until later so Angie agreed to watch him."

"Well I need to get him from her. I can drop him back off when we get done with the pictures. Tell her to give you the address to the church or you can give me her number and I'll call her."

Deena hesitated. Shawn wasn't giving up and she couldn't think of anything else to hold him off.

"I'll call her and let you know."

She saw her grandmother coming back to the car and she pulled one of her earrings out and tucked it in her hand. She got out of the car and walked fast toward her.

"Grandma I think one of my earrings fell out in the bathroom. Go to the car I'll be right back."

Her grandmother walked to the car and she ran into the bathroom to call Angie. The phone rang and went to voicemail.

That was it.

She would tell Shawn Angie wasn't answering her phone. She dialed him back and at the same time, he was calling her again.

"Hello," she said.

"Hey. Is that Stephanie and Ronnie's wedding?"

"I don't know who's wedding it is. She just said she was doing makeup for a wedding today."

"I know this guy Ronnie through my barber. Well, I don't really know him like that, but he said last week that he was getting married this weekend. I wonder if it's the same wedding."

"Well Angie's not answering her phone so I can't find out. I'll try to keep calling her but I'll be driving."

"Okay. I'm about to call my barber and see if he knows where Ronnie's wedding is."

Deena hung up with him and panicked. She knew there was most likely more than one wedding taking place on a Saturday. She had to get Angie to answer the phone. Five minutes had gone by and she still didn't answer. Deena had to think of something to tell her waiting grandmother so she could buy some time. She couldn't talk about it in front of her. She called Angie for the third time.

"Really?! What could this be about?" Angie spoke out loud after hearing the phone ring again.

She asked the bridesmaid to give her a second and she answered the phone.

"Hello."

Deena could hear the hurry in her voice.

"Look. I know you are super busy but it's an emergency." Deena talked fast. "Please tell me that bride and groom isn't Stephanie and Ronnie."

"Yeah. Why? You know them?"

"Oh my God!"

"What's going on?" Angie tried to talk low and stepped out of the ladies' lounge.

"Shawn wants to get Aaron for some damn Christmas photo shoot at his mother's church. I told him he was with you at a wedding and that you were watching him for my aunt. I said you weren't answering your phone, but he is losing his mind over this family picture with his mother and kids."

"So, what's the emergency?" Angie was confused. "Just tell him I never answered my phone."

"He knows the people getting married! And he's probably trying to figure out where the wedding is so he can come and get Aaron from you."

"What?!"

"Yes! I don't know what to do! He told me about the stupid pictures but I forgot."

"Why didn't you just say you didn't know where I was and I wasn't answering my phone?!"

Deena's phone rang again.

"This is him calling back. Hold on."

Deena clicked over.

"Hey I got in touch with my barber. He's invited to that wedding. He made some phone calls and found out that it *is* a girl doing makeup at the church for the bridesmaids. That's Angie so call her and tell her I'll be there to get Xavier."

"Wait!" Deena tried to make one last ditch effort to get him to give up. "Angie's still not answering her phone."

"Listen, I told you about this weeks ago. Whether she answers or not, I'm going over there to get him and I'll take him back to her when I'm done."

It was nothing Deena could do.

"Okay. I'll keep trying to call her anyway." Deena clicked back over to Angie. "I tried but he's on his way to the church," she said sadly.

"Deena! Kayla is here. What am I supposed to tell her? That I'm sending him with a strange man?"

"I don't know! I'm sorry. Maybe tell him you'll bring him out to the car so nobody'll see him. I gotta go. My grandmother's sitting in the car waiting for me. I'll give him your number. Just answer the phone so he won't come walking in there at least."

Deena hung up the phone and called Shawn back. She gave him Angie's number and told him she "finally" answered the phone. Her grandmother had come back into the bathroom.

"You in here on the phone? I thought you were lookin' for your earring."

"I gotta go bye." Deena hung up on Shawn. "I found it grandma."

She held up the earring she still had in her hand.

"That was Angie calling to tell me something."

They headed back to the car and continued the trip. Deena hoped Angie could manage giving Aaron to Shawn discreetly. As long as he stayed in his car no one would notice.

Angie went back to the ladies' lounge. She was on the seventh bridesmaid with just Kayla and the bride left. She worked the makeup brush back and forth on the girl's face trying not to look frustrated. Kayla walked back in with Aaron. She had taken him outside for a few minutes. Angie was so upset by the phone call she hadn't noticed they were gone from the room. She didn't say anything and just kept working. How was she going to get Aaron out of the church without Kayla seeing her? She finished up the last girl before Kayla. She looked down into her bag at her cell phone. It hadn't rang yet and she wondered if Shawn would call first instead of just showing up.

"Is it my turn finally?" Kayla yelled across the room.

Aaron was on her lap with a bottle in one hand and softly pulling his own hair with the other. Angie knew he was getting sleepy.

159

"Yeah, come on," Angie said.

The bridesmaids had started to put their dresses on. Kayla carried Aaron over with her and sat in the makeup chair.

"You gonna hold him while I'm trying to do your face?"

"Yeah. I can hold him across my lap. He's about to fall asleep anyway."

Kayla laid Aaron across her lap. Angie scanned over the makeup kit to choose the right colors for Kayla's skin tone. She could hardly focus thinking of her phone ringing any minute.

"You got business cards? Did you give them your number?"

Kayla told Angie to give the bridal party her information so they could pass it on for other events and weddings.

"Um......yeah I did. Okay hold your face still and tilt your chin up just a little."

Angie started on Kayla's makeup. She glanced over toward the corner of the room to see where all of Aaron's things were. She needed to know what to gather quick when it was time.

And there it was. Her phone rang inside the duffel bag.

"Kayla, go in the bathroom and get me some tissue."

Angie reached for the phone and tried to think fast.

"Why?" Kayla asked.

"I need to tap out some of the powder on my brush and I use tissue."

She knew Kayla wouldn't know one way or the other if this was true. She only wore makeup on special occasions. Angie reached out and took Aaron from her arms, answering the phone at the same time. Kayla walked out of the room to get some tissue.

"Hello."

Angie grabbed Aaron's diaper bag and made her way out with him to the front doors of the church.

"Hey Angie. This is Shawn. Deena gave me your number and……"

"I know." Angie cut him off and walked as fast as she could. "I'm walking outside with him right now. Where are you?"

Shawn had just pulled up.

"I'm parked across the street down a little way from the church. In a gray car."

Angie saw him and hung up taking the phone away from her ear. People were starting to show up and had filled the parking spaces out front. She crossed the street with Aaron grasped in one arm. Shawn stepped out of the car.

"I'm sorry for interrupting you but thank you so much for letting me get him."

"That's okay. I'll be back home around five so you can just bring him back to me."

She needed to keep the conversation short and get back into the church before anyone saw her. She turned around to walk back across the street.

"I need his car seat," Shawn called out to her.

"Oh shoot! It's in my car. I'll run and get it."

Her heart beat fast.

"How could I forget the stupid car seat?! Of course, this became the plan all of a sudden," she said to herself. "It was left in the car for a reason. Because I was supposed to be going back home with my son, not him going with somebody else."

She got the car seat and headed back toward Shawn. Her feet pressed all the way forward in her heels patting against the ground from running. She handed him the car seat and turned to run back into the church. She looked up and Kayla was standing on the front steps.

She had seen everything.

CHAPTER 22

Deena consumed herself with Angie having to give Aaron to Shawn. She had planned on making the best of the trip and bonding more with her grandmother. By the time they made it to the small country town, she had heard all about how Kayla was in on their secret. Angie told her how she got caught handing Aaron over and Kayla of course being Kayla, demanded to know the who, what, and why. Deena and Kayla were cordial with each other in person, but really didn't like each other. Angie sometimes had to hear one make snide comments about the other for whatever reason. When she told Deena that Kayla knew about Shawn, she left out the part about Kayla calling Deena a stuck-up bitch, using Aaron for her self-serving shenanigans. And Angie had to hear from Deena that Kayla was the last person who should know the secret because she was shady, a loud-mouth, and always in Angie's business. Nonetheless, Angie said she swore Kayla to secrecy. It didn't stop Deena from being nervous about it. She still didn't trust Kayla. This was something she and Angie would take to their graves.

It gave her a little comfort knowing Kayla had

to realize Angie was just as at fault as she. It was Angie's dirty little secret too. Deena was more pissed at Shawn. If it wasn't for him insisting that his overbearing mother have her way for some stupid Christmas pictures, no one would know. Luckily Kayla didn't know Shawn. If she ever wanted to tell all, she'd have to find him first. Deena pushed through the rest of the trip but worried about her situation, not knowing how to make it right.

She made the drive home with her grandmother and the little rental car was filled with stuff she brought back. Deena's great aunt bagged and boxed up keepsakes from her bedroom closet like she was giving them to Goodwill. She had even gone out to her backyard shed and got stuff from an old trunk. Some of it clicked and clacked around in the backseat when Deena went over bumps. A picture frame wasn't packed well and slid from side to side in another box. It all smelled of a liniment and mothballs mixed with something rain-soaked from outside. Deena regretted making the trip every time she inhaled. She managed to keep from vomiting by cracking some of the windows open every now and then. Her grandmother complained of too much wind and the fact that it was winter, didn't help. It was too cold to drive with windows cracked open. Her grandmother didn't seem bothered by the smell of the stinky gifts from her dear sister-in-law and Deena was at least thankful that she had to make frequent stops for her to use the bathroom. She could catch some fresh air and not vomit all over the steering wheel while driving.

At one of their many stops at a full-service gas station, Deena saw plastic tarps for sale stacked near the door. She bought one hoping to cover the stuff in the backseat and smother the awful smell. While her grandmother was using the bathroom inside, she pulled the tarp apart and it was way too large for the backseat of a car. Deena didn't care as long as she covered that smell. She spread the plastic over the bags and boxes, tucking the leftover parts underneath and around the sides to create a seal. She closed the car door and stood back, looking at her work through the window.

She rolled her eyes.

When the car was first packed it looked like she and her grandmother were homeless and living out of it. It looked even worse with the overflowing plastic covering stuff in the entire backseat.

"Rather that, than throw up driving," Deena said to herself.

She sat in the car to test out the tarp. She smelled nothing but plastic. It worked. Her phone rang and it was Shawn. What did he want now? Deena looked toward the door. She could answer quickly before her grandmother came out. Christmas was five days away and she was sure that's what he was calling about.

"Hello," she spoke quick, watching the door.

"Hey. It's me. I was calling to see what the plan is for Xavier on Christmas."

Deena already had an answer prepared.

"We're gonna do Christmas Day at my aunt's house. My grandmother and the rest of my family are gonna be there."

Her grandmother had come out and was heading to the car.

"Why, what's up?"

"You sound like you're busy," he said.

"Well, I'm about to start driving again and I can't talk while I'm driving."

"Okay I just wanted to say I'll bring his gifts over on Christmas Eve."

"That's fine. We'll be home."

Deena's grandmother had opened the car door and sat inside.

"Did you see those little rock 'n' roll---."

Deena put the phone slightly off her ear and held up one finger at her.

"Oh, I didn't know you were on the phone," her grandmother said.

Deena put the phone back to her ear. Shawn was talking.

"What did you say? I'm sorry I didn't hear the first part."

"I said she's thinking I want to have him over with the kids and she just wants it to be us at the house for Christmas."

She was his wife. It was always *she* if he mentioned her. He probably thought it would burn Deena's ears if he referred to her as *my wife*.

Deena didn't care what she thought about Christmas Day. There was no way Aaron would be with Shawn on Christmas day anyway. Shawn just didn't know that. Deena couldn't help but think for a second what she'd say to Shawn if Aaron was her real son. She would give him a few choice words about his wife not having to worry about her son ever being at their house because he wouldn't be.

"Okay. Whatever."

She rolled her eyes. She hoped he wouldn't say much more. She couldn't talk with her grandmother in the car.

"Okay, I'll call you when I'm on my way," he said.

They hung up. Deena wasn't sure if he noticed the attitude in her voice or if he just ignored it. She put the phone in the middle console and put on her seat belt.

"Who was that?" Her grandmother asked.

"Huh?"

Deena knew she may ask who was on the phone because her nosiness always got the best of her.

"I asked who was that on the phone?"

"Oh. Somebody from my job."

Deena started driving. The bags and boxes in the backseat shuffled under the tarp. The small Hyundai Accent she rented was hard to the road and made it worse. It was almost like a crunchy plastic sound. She could still hear the unproperly packed picture frame click inside one of the boxes. At least that awful smell was covered.

"Why'd you say we'll be home? They're asking about when we're getting home?"

Deena didn't think she heard that part. She wanted to tell her nosy grandmother it was none of her business but she could still be backhanded by her even as a grown woman. It was something that just couldn't be said to an old-school woman from the south.

She had to lie again.

"I didn't say we'll be home. I said *I'll* be home."

"Oh."

Her grandmother opened her purse and took out her glasses. She had placed a Reader's Digest in the pocket of the car door and picked it up to read. She hadn't even noticed the crinkling tarp.

CHAPTER 23

It was unusual for Angie to be asleep at one o'clock in the afternoon. She had worked all week since the wedding and agreed to work someone else's hours the following Saturday, giving up her off day. Tia was with her dad and after Angie dropped off Aaron at day care, she got a call from the girl who needed her to work, saying she didn't need the day off anymore. Angie thought hard about going back to get Aaron, but decided she'd sleep in for half the day first. She needed a little *me* time. She stepped out of a hot bath and dried herself off only to put on loungewear and climb into bed. She pulled her big favorite purple comforter up to her chin and fell asleep to a movie. She was lightly snoring with her body wrapped tight in the covers like a cocoon. Her head was even covered.

She eventually woke up to the sound of light tapping, but put the covers back over her head after a few seconds of not hearing it anymore. It came again. This time louder. She pulled the cover off her head and let out of whiny growl. She got up ready to tell whoever it was that they had the wrong apartment and slam the door. Her hair was wild and part of it still stood up on her head from the cover being violently pulled off. She went to the door quickly and looked through the peephole.

It was her mother!

Angie frowned so hard her entire face wrinkled. What did she want? And how did she even know where she lived? She thought about ignoring her and pretending she wasn't home. She turned around and put her back against the door.

"What the fuck?!" She whispered to herself.

It could only be Kayla to blame for her showing up. Angie knew she was the only one to tell her where she lived. She looked around the room. Her apartment was a mess. She was a mess. It was not the time to have a mother-daughter moment. Her mother was too snobbish for that anyway. She contemplated going quietly back to her bed when her mother lightly tapped on the door again.

"Angie, it's me. Your mother."

Angie rolled her eyes. Her mother had to know she was home. She turned around to face the door and used her hands to brush her hair up around the edges into her messy bun. Kayla was definitely to blame. Whatever it was, she wanted to get it over with and go back to bed. She opened the door and stared at her without saying a word. It had been four years since they'd spoken and that was at Kayla's father's funeral.

Her mother hadn't changed a bit. A large yellow Prada bag hung over her shoulder and she wore a black dressy long sleeve jumpsuit with high heel boots. It could be nine o'clock in the morning and she'd be dressed that way. Angie was pretty sure she didn't own a pair of gym shoes and she couldn't even remember a time seeing her in a pair of jeans. Certain clothes just didn't make her feel as "important" as others. Gym shoes and jeans didn't turn heads as far as she was concerned. Her makeup was caked on too. She always overdid it. Angie looked down and saw her holding two big Macy's bags.

"Hey. I hope you don't mind me coming by but I wanted to see you and the kids. It's been a long time."

She stood there holding the bags with a desperate look.

"Why?"

Angie couldn't help but wonder where this was coming from all of a sudden. She stood still in the doorway.

"Angie!" Her mother acted like she didn't understand the dismissive response. "I wanna try to have a better relationship. I realize I'm mostly to blame for that."

Her voice went to almost a whisper. She was still standing in the hallway because Angie hadn't invited her in. Angie was shocked to see her so vulnerable. Her pride was always bigger than she was, and she wasn't the type to admit she was wrong about anything.

Her face softened.

What had gotten into her snotty mother? Angie thought for sure she had some sort of terminal illness and she wanted to right all her wrongs. She was selfish and never did anything for anyone unless it served her in some way.

"Look, if you just want me to leave I will. But I brought you and the kids something." She held out the two bags to Angie. "If you don't want yours, will you at least let them have theirs?"

Angie took the bags and stepped backward inside the apartment.

"You can come in. Thank you."

She still sounded upset. She pushed some of Aaron's toys out of the way toward the kitchen.

"Excuse the mess," she said without making eye contact.

"It's fine Angie. Where are the kids? I really want to see the baby. I heard he's getting big."

She sat down on the couch.

"Tia's at school and Aaron's at daycare. I had the day off and needed a break so I was sleeping in for a while."

Angie opened the blinds a little to let some light in.

"Oh, I'm sorry I interrupted you. I know how it is to get that time to crawl back in bed. I won't stay long."

Angie sat down on the other couch across from her.

"That's okay. I have a little more time before I have to pick up Aaron."

Her mother saw his picture by the TV and went over and picked it up. She stared at it. She told Angie how cute he was and that she couldn't wait to see him and Tia.

"Your Aunt Marie told me their sizes and I went and got them some things. Look at them and make sure they'll fit okay."

Angie opened the bag and held up the clothes. They were shorts and pants for Aaron and some dresses and tops for Tia. She still didn't know what emotion to have with her mother suddenly showing up and being nice. Her mother seemed to be interested in her. She asked about her job and future plans. Angie got excited and she said she was hoping to one day start a business doing makeup. She caught her own heightened tone of voice and brought it back down. She stayed cordial but never smiled. She was still guarded. Her mother had shunned her for getting pregnant at eighteen and they hadn't spoken in years. It would take more than a pop-up visit to rekindle the relationship. Angie didn't feel they ever really had one in the first place. Ever since she was a kid, everything was always so formal and fake and all about putting on a show in front of people. Only time would tell if her mother had changed her ways. Angie was grown of course and didn't have to put on a façade. She wasn't going to allow her kids to be put through that either. She patiently listened to her mother for another half hour without talking much herself. Her mother could tell her sudden company wasn't wanted. She grabbed onto the handles of her purse sitting next to her on the couch.

"Well, I'll get out of here and let you catch some more sleep."

She stopped and reached around in her purse. She took out an old receipt and an ink pen.

"Marie gave me your address and phone number. Can I call you? I'm leaving mine here so you'll have it."

She sat the receipt on the table. Angie didn't answer right away.

"Come on Angie. I just want to be able to see the kids sometimes. They *are* my grandkids and I want them to know me."

"Mom, you've had a granddaughter all these years and she's seven. Where have you been all this time for a relationship with *her*?"

"That's my fault I know. But I wanna put that behind me and not do the same thing with Aaron." She stood up and threw her purse over her shoulder. "Will you at least let me see them? I understand if you don't want to be around me yourself. Just give me a chance to be a grandmother to them."

"That's fine."

Angie looked up at her for a second and then looked away. She didn't say anything else.

"And of course, it can be on your terms. I'll call you soon to see what your schedule is," her mother said walking to the door.

Angie stood up to lock the door behind her.

"Thank you for the clothes."

"You're welcome. You have something in the other bag."

Her mother pointed to a small gold bag on the couch where Angie had been sitting. Angie never looked in it.

"Okay. Thank you," she said plainly.

She locked the door and looked at the bag on the couch. It was under one of the Macy's bags. Angie had taken it out of the bag and sat it next to her on the couch. She picked it up and pulled out a two-pack gift set of facial cleaner and lotion. It was from the makeup section at Macy's. There was also a $25 gift card with it. Her mother wrote something on the under flap of it that read:

I found out makeup is your specialty. I hope you like this.

Love,
Mom.

Angie stood in place holding the card in her hand. Her mother had obviously inquired about her to her Aunt Marie and Kayla. They both wanted them to have a better relationship but they knew her mother was to blame. She sometimes estranged herself from the rest of the family and only showed up when there was a funeral. When it came to Angie, they thought it was overkill that she stopped speaking to her for getting pregnant young. Angie sat the bag on the table and grabbed her phone to call Kayla.

"Hello."

"Remind me to smack you when I see you," Angie said to her.

"What?"

"For telling my mother where I live."

Angie held the phone out from her ear and spoke into the mouthpiece.

"I didn't tell her. My mom did."

"Hmmm. I wonder who told *your* mom so she could tell mine. Aunt Marie doesn't know where I live. She said she got it from Aunt Marie, but I didn't believe her."

"Yeah, my mom asked me for your address the other day but I didn't know why. What happened?"

"She popped up at my house! I was sleeping in for a while and she was the last person I wanted showing up at my door."

Angie plopped down on her bed still upset.

"Well, I'm guessing you let her in, right? How'd it go?"

"Yeah, I let her in. She brought the kids some new clothes. I'm just wondering what she's up to. I don't trust her."

"Oh, stop being difficult. At least she reached out to you. Maybe she sees the error of her ways."

Kayla tried convincing Angie to give her mother a chance.

"You know how to keep her at bay until she proves herself. Just see how it goes," Kayla said.

"Yeah, well it's going to be on my terms. I guess I can't be mad at Aunt Marie for giving her my address. That *is* her sister and she's always wanted her to come down off her high horse and get over me getting pregnant at eighteen."

"She'll be happy to know you two exchanged pleasantries," Kayla giggled.

She was being funny.

"Shut up. I'll talk to you later."

Angie put the phone down on her nightstand and climbed back in bed. She'd wait two more hours to pick up Aaron. She pulled the covers over her head and fell back to sleep.

CHAPTER 24

January 2nd was always the day Angie took her Christmas tree down. She had a small 4-foot one in the corner of the living room. Her decorating theme was the same every year. She hung pictures of the kids all over it with gold and silver pipe cleaners threaded through each one to make it an ornament. Before Aaron was born, she hung pictures of her and Tia.

She pulled each picture off carefully, keeping the pipe cleaner attached and placed them in a box for the next year. She watched Aaron and worked quickly to wrap the lights in a coil before he gained interest. He stood still focused on a cartoon on TV. If he noticed her, she would have to pry things from his hands. When she decorated the tree, he somehow got hold of the end of the lights twice and pulled, making the whole tree fall. She even had to pry some of the pictures from his hands because he had bent them. Toys were always around the living room but he was somehow interested in whatever she was doing. Tia was home and could help keep him occupied.

They were both dressed and ready to go. Angie's mother had asked if she could take them to the mall for a few hours. She was sick through Christmas and couldn't shop for their gifts. Angie mustered up enough empathy to go out to eat with her a few days after she showed up at the apartment. She took the kids with her and her mother was ecstatic. She held Aaron on her lap most of the time and managed to get through a conversation with Tia as he banged a toy up and down on the table. Angie was impressed at how she bonded with them and didn't mind Aaron making a mess all around her.

She asked Angie about her plans for Christmas. Angie usually went to her Aunt Marie's and celebrated with her and Kayla. She and Brian agreed to switch having Tia each year, and it was her year. Angie told her she and the kids were staying home for a change and celebrating together. She knew her mother would sometimes come by Marie's on Christmas but wouldn't stay long. She and Marie exchanged gifts and she'd leave, but Angie hadn't seen her there for the past couple of years.

Angie circled her straw around in her soda at the table. Her mother hadn't said what her plans were or what she had done for the past two years. Angie didn't ask. After seconds of awkward silence, she got up to use the bathroom. She gave Tia instructions on distracting Aaron until she came back.

"He'll be fine Angie. He's focused on making a mess with the fries," her mother said laughing.

Aaron was swiping his fries across the high chair tray. Her mother had put him in it and off her lap

once the food was served. Angie headed to the bathroom. She was seeing a different side to her mother.
Having a down-to-earth relaxed personality was not
her. She seemed genuinely happy to be around the
kids. Angie thought about when she asked to have
a chance to be their grandmother. She wanted them
to know her as long as she had changed her ways.
She used the bathroom and washed her hands, looking at herself in the mirror. She stared. It had been a
ten-year rift between them. She didn't want to be the
reason her kids didn't see their grandmother. At least
they could have the best of both worlds. She left the
bathroom and headed back to the table. Aaron was
drinking from his sippy cup. She slid back into the
booth next to Tia and sat down.

"Do you mind if I drop their gifts off on Christmas
since you'll be home?" Her mother asked. "That'll
be the only Christmas shopping I gotta do."

"Umm…no. I don't mind," Angie said.

She didn't expect her mother to ask that.

"Now I'm gonna have even more stuff for
Christmas!" Tia said loudly.

She was excited about it, but Angie didn't like
Tia getting her hopes up in case her mother was a
no-show.

On Christmas she didn't show, but she wasn't
a no-show. She had been sick over the next several
days and confined to her apartment. She stayed in
touch with Angie, but insisted she and the kids didn't
try to visit. She was afraid of getting them sick.

Angie could hear it in her voice that she had come down with something. She begged Angie to let her take the kids shopping when she got well. Tia had been anxious to get gifts from her. Tia was just happy to get gifts period. The more, the better. She stood in the living room window watching for her to come.

Angie pulled the plastic branch sections off the tree one by one and placed them in a small pile to pack away. Aaron had come over and reached into her picture ornaments.

"Tia! You're supposed to be watching him for me."

Angie grabbed his hand and took a picture from it.

"Oh sorry," Tia said. She turned around from staring out the window. "I'm watching for grandma to pull up."

"She's coming Tia. You don't have to stand in the window. She's gonna come to the door."

Tia looked around the living room for one of Aaron's toys.

"Come on Aaron."

She picked up his blue bouncy ball and threw it up in the air, taking his attention away from the decorations.

"And remember what I told you," Angie said. "Don't let him out of your sight today. And you know the number to call me if something happens."

"Yes," Tia said, still throwing up the ball.

The doorbell rang. Tia dropped the ball and ran to

the front window. She could see her grandmother's car parked on the street. Angie walked out to open the lobby door for her. Her fancy long black suede coat hung down to her ankles with each big shiny button secured all the way to her neck. A black chenille winter beret sat carefully on her head, placed perfectly so not to mess her hair up. An off-white scarf matched her high-heeled, pointed-toe boots. Angie looked her up and down.

"Tia is excited, just so you know. She...um." Angie paused. "You sure you're dressed for handling a one-year-old at the mall?"

She stared at her boots.

"Well, the mall has the little kiddie push carts. I'm gonna put him in one of those, but it'll be a one stop shop and then I'm taking them to the toy store."

"Oh okay," Angie said. "I was gonna say, I feel for you," she laughed.

"You forgot you were a one-year-old once too." Her mother gave her a side eye. "I know what I'm doing." She looked at Tia. "Besides, I got you right?"

"Yes," Tia said with a grin from ear to ear.

"Between the two of us, we can handle Aaron."

Tia shook her head in agreement. Angie was putting on Aaron's coat. Tia held his hand to head out the door.

"Remember what I told you," Angie said to her. "Behave."

"Yes," Tia said.

Angie gave her a look to remind her of what they

talked about earlier. The "behave" part was not to let on to her mother that she meant something else.

"Okay, I'll bring them back in a few hours. We're gonna stop and get something to eat too," her mother said.

Angie handed her Aaron's car seat.

"Okay, I'll be here. Have fun."

Angie closed the door and watched them walk down the front walkway to the car. She was still getting used to this "new mother" of hers. She finished packing away her Christmas stuff and took it down to her basement storage locker. She came back upstairs to find Deena tapping on her door.

"I was just trying to call you."

"I took my tree and stuff down to the basement."

Angie stepped in front of her and unlocked her door.

"What you up to?" Deena asked, following her inside.

"Nothin."

"How was it with your mom and the kids?"

"They just left."

Angie grabbed a bowl of popcorn from the kitchen and sat on the couch.

"They should be okay."

She told Deena about how she gave Tia strict instructions for watching Aaron and to call her if something happens.

"Geez girl," Deena teased her. "You act like she's gonna kidnap 'em or somethin."

She laughed. Angie stuffed her mouth with popcorn and had to wait to talk.

"She's just so bourgeois. She wasn't even dressed to handle him. Wearing high heel boots."

Angie looked at Deena and rolled her eyes at the thought.

"You know how your mom is," Deena said shaking her head.

She walked over to Angie and got a handful of popcorn from the bowl. She sat on the opposite end of the couch and ate one piece at a time from her hand. Angie's phone rang and Deena passed it to her. It was Kayla. She had called earlier that morning asking to use the car again. Another "Derrick trip out of town" with their car. Angie sighed with irritation at seeing that it was her calling.

"It's Kayla," she told Deena. "Hello."

"Hey, I'm coming to the door."

Derrick was dropping her off. Angie forced a handful of popcorn into her mouth and brushed her hands together to get rid of the crumbs.

"Is she at the door?" Deena asked.

She could tell Angie was about to go the door by how she quickly ended the call and stood up.

"Yeah. Coming to use my car again of course."

Deena rolled her eyes and stood up to leave. She couldn't stand Kayla.

"Don't leave," Angie said. "She is only coming to get the car."

Angie opened the apartment door and stepped

into the hallway. Deena slowly sat back down on the couch. She hoped it would be quick. Kayla came into the hallway stomping the snow off her boots before stepping inside.

"Hey, what's up?" She spoke to Deena.

"Hey," Deena said.

Deena reached for the remote and channel surfed. Angie had gone into the bedroom to get her spare car key.

"Where's the kids?" Kayla yelled from the living room.

Angie walked out and handed her the key.

"With my mom. To get their Christmas gifts."

"Oh yeah. She called my mom and told her," Kayla said. "My mom said she was excited."

Angie sat back on the couch and grabbed her popcorn. Deena stared at the TV to avoid the conversation.

"You sure you don't have to go anywhere today?"

"Nope. I'm about to watch a movie while the kids aren't here."

"Okay. I'll bring the car back in the morning."

Kayla left and Angie locked the door behind her.

"Don't tell me her man is going out of town again?" Deena said giving Angie a serious look.

"Yeah. I guess. I don't know how somebody that won't work has the luxury of going out of town whenever they feel like it," Angie said.

"No job. That's how."

They both laughed.

"I don't know what they got going on. I don't get in her business."

Angie thought about Bruce and her own situation.

"I can't talk about anybody. I got pregnant by a lyin', no-job having bastard who left me high and dry with the baby." Angie laughed. "I'm in no position to judge."

Deena didn't say anything. She knew Angie was right. But Angie was always bad at picking men. She reminded her of it.

"Girl you complain now, but after Brian you went for the bad boys and *only* the bad boys," Deena said.

"Well, I'm done now. No more bad boys for me. So, you watchin' this movie with me or not? I'm trying to get it in before my kids get back."

Angie grabbed the remote to change the channel to what the movie was on.

"And it's about to start."

Deena walked over and grabbed the popcorn bowl from her.

"Yup. I'm in," she said.

They watched an entire almost three-hour suspense movie Angie had always heard was good, but never got to see it. They were in the middle of debating something said between two characters when her mother came back with Tia and Aaron.

"Right on time," Angie said wide-eyed looking at Deena. "Finally got my movie in with no interruption."

She got up and opened the door. Her mother was

carrying Aaron. He had fallen asleep in the car and was still sluggish. Tia came in behind her with a big bag and sat it on the floor. She took stuff out of it excited for Angie to see.

"Mama, look what I got!"

Angie's mother, still sharp from head to toe, asked if she could help get Aaron's things from the car. Deena volunteered and took off her house slippers, stepping her feet into some of Angie shoes by the door. They always wore the same size.

Tia pulled out a girl's jewelry box she picked out at the mall.

"I ended up taking her to the mall for that store, but we got most of the stuff from the toy store," her mother explained.

Tia remembered something.

"Oh, mama. We saw a guy that said he knows Aaron's dad and he saw Aaron at a wedding."

Deena stopped just as she opened the door to go out. She turned around and looked at Angie. Angie looked right back. Deena had to know what was said. She stood in place waiting.

"What'd he say?" Angie asked before Tia or her mother could get a word out. "Did he say Aaron's name?"

"No. He just said he remembered seeing him at a wedding a few weeks ago and he knows his dad," her mother said.

"Okay." Angie was a little relieved. Aaron *was* memorable. His big bushy afro hair made him stand out.

"I did makeup at a wedding and had him with me," Angie said.

She hoped her mother wouldn't ask anything further about it. She hadn't told her anything about Aaron's real dad and she surely wasn't going to mention the fake one either.

"I told grandma that his dad used to be at our house, but left and didn't come back," Tia interjected.

She was referring to Bruce. Angie had told her that before Aaron was born.

"Well, we won't talk about that right now," Angie said quickly.

She didn't need her judgmental mother having an opinion about her son having an in-the-wind father.

CHAPTER 25

Aaron had grown much bigger over the next several months. He was coming up on his second birthday. Angie couldn't stick with the tradition of waiting until a boy turned two before cutting his hair. She had a kids' barber trim his wild afro down to his short wavy roots. He was an even more handsome toddler with mixed features of her and Bruce. Angie was still glad he didn't have *all* Bruce's features since he wasn't around. She wondered if Shawn or his family noticed his looks. They had to. He spent a lot of time with them over spring and summer. He traveled to different places on trips, family reunions, and even to Disney World. He was used to them. Whoever "them" was. Angie had no idea. Other than the occasional bruise or two toddlers get from a fall, he never came back home badly hurt. She couldn't complain about that. Deena told her he answered to "Xavier." He was used to it being around Shawn and his family. Angie called him it once to see for herself, and he turned around and looked at her.

He had learned he had two names. Or so he thought. Angie thought of it as a child having a nickname, but learning to answer to his real name as well.

It helped her to cope with it. She was happy that she taught him to say *mama.* He called her that, but had learned "daddy" from Shawn. Deena was "Dee-ah" in his toddler speech. He couldn't be told to call her mama too. Angie would have it no other way and Deena agreed, but knew it was against how she wished things could go. Shawn caught on to it, hearing him enunciate it in his own way one day when he handed Deena his sippy cup for more juice. He didn't like what he heard.

"Is he calling you Deena?" he asked.

"Yeah. He started doing it after hearing other people say it," she said.

It was the best she could do for an explanation of why her son wasn't calling her mama. She told Shawn she didn't have a problem with it and that she had allowed it for too long to teach him any different. Shawn was obviously baffled at how his son had learned to call him daddy fairly quickly, but his mother made no effort to teach him to call her mama. Deena read his mind in that moment and could sense the confusion. It was the same with Aaron's medications. He got eczema on his legs and neck from the dry summer heat and his pediatrician prescribed a cream for it. Deena tore his name off the label before he went with Shawn. When he asked about it, she used the excuse that she was "paranoid" about people having his prescription information.

"Who would be able to do something with a baby's medication?" He asked.

"I don't know. That's just me. I'm weird about stuff like that."

She left it at that.

Angie remembered to follow suit and she always ripped his name off the label whenever she got any of his medicine refilled at the drug store.

———·«(»·———

Shawn still paid for Aaron's daycare every two weeks. He gave Deena the money and she always gave it to Angie. There was no cost for days Aaron didn't attend. Shawn didn't know that and still paid the same to Deena. No matter what, she still gave the money over to Angie. They both benefited for the most part. Angie sometimes shared with her when she'd have to get her car fixed or when she went to after work dinners with co-workers.

Shawn took over his uncle's transport company and had become pretty well-off for himself. He was able to help his wife open her own salon. She wouldn't have any thoughts of leaving again, trying to partner with someone else to do it. He happily told Deena about taking over the transport company and being his own boss. He never mentioned buying his wife the salon. Deena found out about it after walking into it one day for an eyebrow wax. She noticed it was a new place near her doctor's office and stopped in. *L's HAIR SALON* was the name. His wife's name was Lena. Shawn said it a couple of times when he mentioned her. Deena immediately noticed her and turned and walked out. She never forgot what she looked like from that winter night at her front door. She asked Shawn about it by pretending to know someone who got their hair done there. He told her it *was* his wife's salon and she recently opened it after he took over the transport company.

Deena had her moments of jealousy and that was one of them. She still had flashbacks of when she and Shawn were together and he was the man she always wanted. Someone else had him all along and she hated it. She hated *her*.

It gave Deena solace making her think her husband fathered a child with another woman. It was nothing worse for a woman to have to bear. Deena had become that person. At times she didn't care about the web she tangled for herself and everyone involved. She thought there was no way out so she'd improvise and try to be ready at every turn for what came next.

Aaron had already learned to say words and Angie and Deena knew he'd be school age soon. They talked about Deena moving out of state and leaving Shawn to wonder, but that wouldn't work. Angie couldn't leave with her and someone was bound to run into her and Aaron somewhere in the city. It would all come out and Angie would have to fear the worst while Deena got off scot free living somewhere else. Besides, Shawn had become so attached to Aaron and rightfully so, that he'd go to the ends of the earth to find him.

Aaron benefited a great deal from Shawn becoming the owner of his own company. He always came home with expensive clothes and lots more toys. Shawn even bought him a new three-stage solid oak bed from Pottery Barn Kids. The price tag on it was $1200. It had to stay at Deena's apartment of course. Shawn set it up for Aaron in her second bedroom. She had bought a baby crib from a rummage sale when he was a baby. It was only to make Shawn think he really slept in it. She sat it to the side to make room for the new one. Toys overcrowded the room and Aaron hadn't played with a lot of them. Angie didn't want him getting attached to the oversized ones and have them overcrowd her apartment. Neither, she or Deena had the room for all of them. Deena stuffed a lot of them in the second bedroom closet and donated them whenever she could. Shawn spoiled him. His mother did too. He told Deena one day that he started each of his kids their own college savings account. There was an account out there with the name *Xavier Buchanan*. Shawn didn't know he was just building an extra savings for his other kids because Xavier Buchanan didn't exist.

Him becoming more well-off made things worse. He made his own work hours and didn't work on weekends anymore. He wanted to get Aaron every other weekend and had completely stopped visiting him at Deena's apartment. He was taking him away for every visit and bringing him back. Deena had run out of excuses for why he couldn't go so she relented, and every other Saturday became the norm for the most part.

CHAPTER 26

It didn't take long for Angie to get some clients who needed her for their wedding party makeup. The business cards she made certainly got the word around. She still worked at the mall kiosk, but some of her summer weekends were spent with bridal parties. She started to hate being out in the open at the mall. She applied for the cosmetic counter at Nordstrom hoping to get tucked away from the everyday crowd. She didn't tell the kiosk owner that she applied for a store fifty feet away. She wanted to wait to see if she'd ever get an interview. She cruised in there a few times on a break to see the makeup, but more so to see who worked there.

It was always the same girl.

She was a way too overdone blonde who didn't blend blushes and eyeshadows well on her own face. She wore too much cover and the powder made her look clownish. Angie was sure she scared most people off from asking her advice on makeup. She strongly believed the person working the makeup counter anywhere should have good looking makeup on to attract customers. It was a must.

It was Thursday and sure to be busy at the mall.

Angie was there until closing from one to nine o'clock. She made her way to the kiosk and joined her two co-workers. She wasn't surprised to see people around the stand. Makeup bags and mirrors had been put on sale and a lot were bought with the makeup. She jumped right in and started helping people. One of her co-workers checked out her last customer, ending her shift. Angie and one other girl had to finish out the rest of the day. When it got busy, three people were more helpful, but the two of them managed it. Angie became good at multi-tasking so she could answer questions for people who were undecided while also checking someone out at the register.

The rush had finally started to die down and Angie was showing a customer the different makeup bags to choose from for traveling. She took one and unzipped it to show her the inside. She heard someone say hello to her.

It was Toni, Deena's cousin.

"Hey. How are you?"

Being in the open mall had its pros and cons. Angie saw people she hadn't seen in a while, but she also saw people she didn't necessarily want to see. She was good with seeing Toni. She just had to keep from thinking winter green dresses in summer.

"I'm good," she said. Angie saw her suddenly get a sour look. "Why didn't my cousin tell anybody she had a baby?"

Angie was dumbfounded. How the hell did Toni

find out about Aaron if Deena didn't tell her? She hesitated, not knowing what to say. She couldn't make it seem like it was a total secret. No one had a baby without anybody knowing.

"Why'd you ask that? People know."

"I'm her cousin on her father's side. *None* of us knew."

Toni still had the same sour look. Angie was curious. She asked Toni how she found out.

"My husband's cousin got married back in December and they both go to the same barber as her son's father."

"That damn wedding," Angie thought.

It was the second time someone mentioned it. She hated that she had to give Aaron to Shawn that day. It came back to bite her and Deena big time. There was no telling how many other people knew. Toni went on before Angie could respond.

"And he said her baby was with you in the ladies lounge because you did the bridal party makeup and you were babysitting for her. And the only reason why I know it was Deena is because he showed my husband a picture of her and a picture of the baby. And my husband recognized her."

Angie kept her cool and didn't look shocked. She was still annoyed at how news traveled.

"Boy how the details of other people's business get around," she said sarcastically.

"You know how everybody knows everybody," Toni said. "I haven't been able to catch up with her so she can explain herself. I got a new phone and my contacts didn't transfer over from the old one. Can you give me her number?"

Angie picked up her cell phone from the shelf under the register. She held it up to Toni showing her the screen.

"I would but my phone died a little while ago and I don't have my charger with me. I don't know her number by heart."

Angie's phone was working just fine. If she pushed her home screen button, it would've come on. She pretended it was dead so Toni wouldn't be able to call Deena. Deena couldn't have known that Toni heard about her having a baby because she would've said something about it. Angie knew she had to get to her first.

"Anyway, I'm probably about to move into the same building as you and her. Y'all still live there, right?"

"Yeah," Angie said.

She couldn't handle more bad news at one time. Her forehead wrinkled and she couldn't hide her look anymore.

"Why?"

"Downsizing for a year to save money for a house."

Toni's husband Lance was getting deployed and they both thought it better if she and their four-year old move into an apartment. They had been renting a house and it was better to save and buy one when he came back home.

"And I found out I know the owner of the building so that's even better," Toni said.

A customer came up and Angie's co-worker was already helping someone else. Angie's heart was beating fast at what she just heard. She had been staring at Toni taking in every word. Toni saw the customer waiting.

"I'll let you get back to work. I'll probably see you and Deena in a few days when I come see the apartment," she said, walking away.

Angie said goodbye. She took a deep breath and focused on the customer as much as she could and then took a break. She grabbed her cell phone and rushed away from the kiosk in the opposite direction of Toni. She called Deena while running up the escalator to sit in the food court.

"Hello," Deena said.

She was at work too. Angie looked around for a seat. She was out of breath from running. "Hello," Deena said again.

"Toni knows about Aaron."

"Toni who!?"

"Your cousin Toni."

"What? How?!"

"And the worst part is, she's about to move in our building in that apartment down the hall from you."

Angie tried to calm herself down and hurried to tell Deena the whole thing. She found a seat in the food court but only had a twenty-minute break.

"Are you serious?!" Deena almost yelled all of her responses.

"Yes. She said she knows the owner." Angie talked quick. "And she knows about Aaron from that wedding. I wish I would've never stepped into that damn church with him."

Angie got choked up but held back her tears.

"I can't believe this. This is too much," Deena said. She stared down at her desk calendar with her head in one hand. She held the phone with the other.

"Okay. What does she actually know?"

"Her husband's cousin was the groom and he and Shawn go to the same barber."

Angie's frown seemed permanent on her face. Her look hadn't changed since Deena answered the phone.

"I guess he told them one day at the barber shop that he had to come and get his son from there and then showed her husband a picture of him and then a picture of you."

"That picture of me is old," Deena said. "He took a picture of me with his phone when we were together. I can't believe he still has it. Oh my God."

Deena kept her head down contemplating what to do next. Someone tapped her on the shoulder. She almost jumped turning around in shock.

"Your call light is blinking. I can see it from my desk."

It was her boss. Deena forgot she placed someone on hold while she checked an order. Angie had called her cell phone and she answered thinking it would be quick.

"Oh yeah I'm sorry. I'm getting it now. I had an emergency call on my cell phone," she said.

Her heart nearly jumped out of her chest. She had to process what Angie told her *and* remember what she was checking for the customer on hold. Her boss walked away.

"Let me call you back."

She hung up with Angie not waiting for her to respond. She picked the call up from hold.

"I'm still checking ma'am. Thanks for holding," she said.

She took a minute to collect her thoughts.

Angie walked back to the kiosk. Her face still had the same frown.

As soon as they got a moment that night to come up with their next plan, Angie and Deena did. It was nothing they could do should Toni move in the building. They couldn't go to the owner and badmouth her to make her look like a fraud who didn't pay her rent, or some type a drama queen nuisance wherever she lived. Toni knew the owner. They didn't know how well, so their claims may not have held any weight with her. Deena's option of moving out didn't work for either of them. They both had renewed one-year leases six months from each other. Deena didn't have to worry about Shawn coming inside the apartment anymore to visit Aaron. She usually just took him to the front lobby door and Shawn took him from there. Now she hated she renewed her lease. Toni was going to *always* be around. They talked about staging Deena's apartment again to make it look like Aaron lived there. It worked with Shawn.

"But what if she pops up at my door?" Deena asked.

She couldn't rule that out. Toni was her cousin and she would feel comfortable just showing up from down the hall. Aaron would be with Angie. Deena knew she'd have to figure out Toni's schedule and sneak Aaron back to Angie whenever she wasn't around.

Angie looked at Deena.

"I feel like I'm spending all my energy now trying to keep this going," she said.

"Me too. Now we gotta watch *everybody*."

It was late and they talked in Deena's apartment. Tia was in bed watching TV and Angie had waited for Aaron to fall asleep before leaving.

While they talked, Deena stared over at a bottle of Beringer wine. She got it months before from a co-worker as a birthday gift. She wasn't much of a drinker so it sat on her counter as a kitchen decoration. Angie still had the frown on her face from earlier. It had for sure turned to concrete.

"That damn wedding," she said.

She couldn't stop saying how she wished she had never gone. She hated she told Kayla she would do the makeup. It was how Kayla found out about Aaron. Now Toni, and there was no telling who else knew. Deena felt bad about it and for not coming up with a better way to keep Shawn away. Angie didn't know anyone there but Kayla. Deena wasn't there, but she wouldn't have known anyone either. All the bridesmaids believed Angie was Aaron's mother. But with Shawn running his mouth about him being his son, all the groomsmen by then thought Angie was just a babysitter. They were both lucky they didn't know anyone at the wedding in that case.

"I'm not worried about them. Shit I'm worried about Toni moving in here," Deena said.

Seeing Toni at her door wouldn't leave her mind.

"But I gave out all those business cards at that wedding," Angie said.

She saw more problems coming besides Toni.

Deena wasn't listening. They had to deal with Toni first, and the rest when it came.

"I got it!" Deena said staring at the floor, not blinking. "I got a temporary fix."

"What?"

"When is your lease up again?"

"Not until February."

"Okay. Let Aaron move in with me. Just for a few of months."

"What?!"

Angie was confused.

"I'm gonna get the money from Shawn for you to break your lease and pay the landlord for four months. That way you can move out sooner and we don't have to worry about Toni seeing you with Aaron. I'll leave as soon as my lease is up next year unless she leaves first."

Angie didn't like it. She hadn't planned on moving anytime soon.

"What is that gonna do? You'll still be here. So that means Aaron will have to stay with you longer than just a few months. Why can't you ask him for what it would be to break *your* lease?"

"I don't wanna have to ask for too much. That's already a lot. Besides, I'll have to come up with a damn good reason for moving to get him to give it to me." Deena looked nervous. "At least you won't be around for her to see him around you. You know he'll end up saying *mama* to you or something and it'll be all over."

Deena knew Toni would run back and tell her husband and Shawn would get the news in no time.

"Well okay genius," Angie said staring at her. "How are we supposed to avoid that until then?"

She still had to look for a place and set a date to move. In the meantime, Toni would already be living in the building.

"I'll just keep him with me most of the time when I'm home and sneak him back to you at night. Once we figure out her schedule and routine, we should be okay."

It was getting late. Angie left and went back to her apartment. Aaron was still asleep. Tia had fallen asleep watching TV. Angie pulled the cover further up on her and quietly turned the TV off. She went to her room and kissed Aaron on the forehead.

Deena was in her apartment leaning her back against the door ever since Angie left. She looked up and over to the bottle of Beringer wine. She poured herself a full glass and downed it. It was almost midnight and no time for sleep. She had to come up with a reason to get the money from Shawn. She grabbed her laptop, opened a blank Word document, and started typing.

CHAPTER 27

Toni's husband had been deployed and she wasted no time moving into the building. It had only been two weeks since she saw Angie at the mall and told her. Angie and Deena were both at work the day she moved in. It was a Tuesday. Deena hadn't been able to ask Shawn for the money because he hadn't picked up Aaron for two weekends straight. He said something about having to fill in until his new hires could start. She had to wait until the coming weekend when he promised to get Aaron. Until then, she and Angie had to be careful around Toni and get a routine for exchanging Aaron when they were home. Deena had even picked Aaron up from daycare on Toni's move-in day. She got off work before Angie and didn't want to run into Toni without having him with her. She could've easily said he was with his dad or someone, but it was a risk in case Toni happened to see him coming in with Angie.

The big moving truck raised Deena's stress level. It was still backed up to the door on the back lawn off the parking lot. TIM'S MOVERS in big red letters was blinding. Toni still wasn't done moving in.

Deena took a deep breath, exhaled and stared at the truck. There was nobody around for the moment. Neither Toni or the movers were in sight.

Deena looked at Aaron in the backseat. He was focused on a toy car that twisted in different directions to change its shape.

"You ready dude?" Deena asked him.

He looked up at her and then back down at the toy car.

"Let's go," she said.

She got him out of the car seat and held his hand quickly walking into the building. They made it upstairs to the apartment door and Deena put her key in the lock.

"So, is this the little cutie you been hidin' from people?"

It was Toni.

Deena nearly jumped. She hadn't even heard her coming. She had been in the basement putting things in her storage space.

"Oh hey! You scared me. I didn't hear you coming," Deena said.

If she had been a few seconds sooner getting her door open, she could've avoided her. "This is Aa.. Xavier." She caught herself. "And no, I'm not hiding my son."

Deena gave her a serious look. She turned the key and opened her door, but stayed in the hall without stepping in. Toni bent down to get a better look at Aaron.

"Hi Xavier. I'm your cousin Toni. You're a handsome little man."

Aaron held his toy car tight and stared back at her.

"Angie told me she saw you and that you were moving here," Deena said. She tried to seem happy.

"Yeah, I got a new phone and lost your number. I tried to call Aunt Jean and I couldn't reach her," Toni said.

Aunt Jean was who Deena stayed with in Georgia.

"Oh."

"Anyway, Angie said her phone had died and she didn't know your number by heart."

"Why aren't you done moving? It's already five o'clock." Deena changed the subject.

"That was the movers' fault. They started late. They have to reimburse me some for that."

Deena could hear people coming up the back stairway.

"Ms. Toni." It was one of the movers. "The baby crib and chair won't fit in the storage," he said standing on the stairs.

"Okay, I'll come down and decide what to switch out," Toni said. She walked away from Deena. "We'll talk later. You still gotta tell me why I didn't know about that cute son of yours. But I'm happy we're neighbors! I'll knock on your door when I'm done," Toni yelled halfway down the stairs.

"Okay." Deena laughed. She went in her apartment and closed the door. "Saved by the bell," she said to herself.

She knew the mover didn't realize how much he was helping the moment. She did not feel like talking to Toni about Aaron right then. She knew it was just going to be best to tell Toni that she had a baby by a married man and was embarrassed. It would explain her not telling her about it. It was much better than telling her Aaron wasn't really her son and she was using him to get revenge on the married man she fell in love with. Nonetheless, not having an excuse at all for hiding the pregnancy and the baby himself made no sense.

Aaron had gone straight to the second bedroom and was in there banging toys around. He knew exactly where Deena kept them. She got him and moved quickly to put him on some pajamas for the evening. Angie had given her some clothes for him. When Toni came back to the door, she'd see Aaron in pajamas. Deena wanted everything to look normal so there were no questions. She'd sneak Aaron back downstairs to Angie later that night. She made him some food and he ate. He speeded back into the bedroom and played, banging the toys around.

Deena heard the hallway go quiet. Toni was finally all moved in. About an hour later, she knocked on Deena's door.

"Really?" She whispered to herself.

It was almost nine o'clock. Aaron was winding down. He always rubbed his eyes whenever he was sleepy. Deena wanted to get him downstairs to Angie before he fell asleep. She was in her nightgown and would pretend they were about to go to bed. She hoped it would get rid of Toni faster. She quietly turned off her living room lamp and kitchen light to make the apartment dark. Only the TV was left on with Aaron watching it on the couch. Deena went to the door and checked the peephole. She opened it.

"Hey. I'm sorry were you in bed already?" Toni asked quietly.

She was still in the same clothes. Her hair looked sweated out pulled back off her face in a ponytail.

"About to go," Deena said. She forced a tired look.

"Damn girl you go to bed early. Well, I never got your phone number earlier. And you still are not off the hook about keeping that precious baby in there a secret."

Aaron got off the couch and walked over to the door by Deena.

"Hey you," Toni waved at him. "My little girl is gonna love to play with you."

Deena knew Toni wasn't giving up on where Aaron came from all of a sudden.

"Like I said earlier, he was not a secret," she said. "Some people knew and some people didn't. I'll tell you why later. Now is not the time because I'm going to bed."

Deena had to pretend some people knew. She would've just invited Toni in and told her right then and there what she had prepared, but she needed to get Aaron downstairs to Angie for bed. She gave

Toni her number and she left and went back to her apartment. Deena closed the door and waited another twenty minutes to make sure she wouldn't knock again for some reason.

Aaron stood in front of the TV. He picked up the remote and was pushing the buttons. The channels were changing and the TV was sounding the error beep over and over.

"Aaron no. Gimme that." Deena took the remote from him. "Come on let's go downstairs to mama," she told him.

She stuffed the clothes he wore there in his bag with his sippy cup. She stepped into her no-back canvas shoes by the door and grabbed him by the hand. They went downstairs and Deena slipped into Angie's apartment quietly with him.

"Did it work?" Angie asked. She was anxious to know.

Aaron was over by the fridge opening it.

"For the most part," Deena said. She felt like some of the hardest part was over. "I still didn't get to tell her how Aaron came along."

She rolled her eyes.

"Let me say *Xavier.*"

"If you do slip up with her and say Aaron, you better say it's his middle name," Angie said.

Deena shook her finger at her in agreement.

"That's a good one. I'll use that."

Aaron had come over from the kitchen with a popsicle in his hand.

"Mama. Pa-sick-o," he said.

He held it out to Angie. He got it from a box of unfrozen ones next to the fridge.

"No, it's too late for that. And it's not a frozen one." Angie took it from him. "It's your bedtime," she told him.

She took a few Ritz crackers out of the box on the table and handed them to him.

"Did he eat?" She asked Deena.

"Yeah, he ate. He went in my fridge asking for popsicles too but I don't have any."

"He loves em. And ice cream too. He thinks ice cream are popsicles," Angie said. "Anything that comes out of the freezer is popsicles."

They both laughed.

They had to repeat the same routine at least for the rest of the week until Aaron left with Shawn. Deena opened Angie's door and listened in the hallway before stepping out to run back upstairs. She slipped quietly back into her apartment without being seen.

CHAPTER 28

Deena got Aaron the next day as planned and headed home with him. She knew Toni would make her way over to be nosy because she had no shame about it. Deena thought about how she would be if her cousin kept it from her that she had a baby. She had to admit to herself that it would be odd. In that case, her excuse to Toni would fit the situation. She didn't care if Toni judged her, as long as she bought it.

"Dee-ah," Aaron called her from the backseat. "Dee-ah. Open dis."

He held out a squishy toy in a plastic package. Deena looked in her rearview mirror at him. She had met Angie at daycare to get him. He wanted her to open his toy. She reached a stoplight and took it from him.

"I have to watch you with this. Don't put this in your mouth," she said to him.

It was a tiny toy that seemed too small for a two-year old. She gave it back to him and watched him squeeze and stretch it. He didn't seem to be pleased at going home with her again. She worried that after a while, he would cry to stay with Angie. Usually, he was just going with her for a short time before Shawn picked him up. It was Wednesday, and Shawn wasn't coming for two more days.

Deena made it home and ran into Toni in the hallway. She was carrying a big box from her basement storage.

"Hey, you need help?"

Deena saw that the box was blocking her view.

"Oh hey," Toni said. The side of her face was pressed against the box. "No, I got it. I'm just gonna sit it right at my door and then push it inside."

She carefully put the box down in front of her apartment.

Aaron stared.

"Hey Xavier," she said smiling and out of breath.

She opened the apartment door.

"I told you I got a playmate for you." Toni called her daughter over to the door. "This is your cousin Jasmine. Jasmine this is Xavier."

They both stared at each other. Jasmine held a spoon with chocolate smear on her lips. A bushy ponytail set atop her head like huge broccoli. She said hi to Aaron with the spoon waving it side to side. He stood there still staring.

"Say hi," Deena said.

He gave a quick wave. He was shy when he met new people.

"She's eating some chocolate cake we got from the store," Toni said. "Come on in. You want some?"

Toni reached for his hand and led him into the

apartment. He made his way around the box in the door and walked in.

"Come on in. I'll get him some cake. Excuse the mess," she said to Deena.

Toni had some unpacked boxes still in the living room and kitchen. Deena stepped in. Toni sat Aaron at her kitchen table next to Jasmine and gave him a piece of cake. Deena made him say thank you and worried about him getting cake before dinner. It was too late to say no. Once a toddler was given sugar, it was no taking it back. Deena didn't want to manage a temper tantrum that soon in front of Toni.

"You still at the same job?" Toni asked.

Deena took her eyes off Aaron cramming cake.

"Yeah, I'm still there." It was a perfect lead into what she was going to say. "Well, I left for almost a year and went and lived with Aunt Jean and Uncle Robert in Georgia," Deena said. "But they gave me my position back when I moved back home."

Toni took DVDs from a box and stacked them neatly under her TV stand. Deena kept talking, but lowered her voice from Aaron and Jasmine.

"I left because I was pregnant with him."

She nodded her head in Aaron's direction. She was telling Toni a similar story to what she told Shawn. She said Shawn was married and she found out after the fact and was embarrassed. She left it at that waiting for Toni's follow-up questions. Toni *always* had follow-up questions.

"What a dirty dog!" Toni said trying to keep her

voice low. "To not tell somebody you're married?!" She looked upset and confused.

"Well yeah I was pissed. I left him alone of course but found out I was pregnant," Deena said.

It made her think back to ringing Shawn's doorbell and his wife answering it.

"And you know what?" Toni went on.

She was giving Deena a look as if she figured something out.

"Lance's cousin said he thought he was married with two kids. He said he remembered him mentioning it one time."

Deena felt like saying that his wife left him and took the kids until things didn't work out for her and she wanted him back all of a sudden. She kept it to herself.

"Well, he stepped up right?" Toni asked. "He was certainly showing off Xavier's picture. *And* yours."

She laughed.

Deena rolled her eyes.

"That was not cool," she said.

"He fell in love with you." Toni half nodded giving Deena a woman-to-woman look. "He's married, had a baby outside his marriage, and was boldly showing people the baby and the mother's picture?!"

Toni stared right at her without blinking.

"Oh please," Deena said. She stared right back at Toni with a serious look. "His wife knows about Xavier. It's out there now so he probably doesn't care who knows. She knows and she stayed with him."

Deena looked over at Aaron making swirls in the bowl with his spoon. She got off the subject and focused on him. Toni had been told enough or too much as it was.

It was time to go.

She started to feel more uncomfortable and wanted to avoid having her know anything else.

"Aa...Xavier, let's go. You should be done."

Deena almost said Aaron again. She told Toni she would get out of her way of more unpacking.

"I gotta make some phone calls before it gets too late," she said.

It was her excuse to leave. Aaron climbed down from the table with his face smeared with chocolate cake like Jasmine. Deena made him say thank you to Toni and wave goodbye to both of them. Aaron turned and looked up at Deena on the way out the door.

"Dee-ah," he said.

Deena ignored him and pulled him by the hand.

"Dee-ah," he said again.

"Is he calling you by your name?" Toni asked. Her eyes widened.

Deena knew it would happen but didn't think it would be so soon. She stayed calm and remembered how she dealt with it when Shawn heard Aaron say it.

"Yeah. I just let him do it," she said in a so-what manner.

She knew Toni's next question.

"Why you let him do that?" Toni looked confused.

"He heard other people say my name and he picked up on it and it stuck. So, I just let him do it."

"Oh, that's different," Toni said.

Deena shuffled Aaron down the hall to her apartment.

"I'll see you later," she said to her while walking away.

Deena stayed at Angie's apartment the next day until it was late enough to go up to her own. She figured if Toni came over, she'd just think she wasn't home yet. She was sure Toni wouldn't come down to Angie's place. Toni didn't call Deena's phone either. She had made Toni think she went to bed at least by nine, so she didn't have to worry about her coming after that. Aaron had fallen asleep and it was good for him to be home all evening. Deena decided to stay at Angie's a couple of times a week for his sake.

———— «()» ————

The weekend couldn't come fast enough. Shawn was coming to pick up Aaron and Deena could ask him for the money to break Angie's lease. She hadn't talked to him in two weeks and she planned on asking him in person. She needed to do it that way. Angie was at work so she had Aaron anyway. She was nervous about asking for so much money but from what she planned to tell him, she hoped it would work. There was no other way to get Angie out before Toni suspected anything.

She had Aaron all ready to go with his weekend bag packed. It was almost ten o'clock and she had just gone downstairs to get him from Angie before she left for work. She thought Toni was either gone or still sleeping. She was nowhere in sight.

Shawn rang the doorbell and she ran down to let him in. Aaron stood at the top of the stairs and looked down.

"X-Man!" Shawn said excited to see him.

It had been three weekends. Aaron giggled and was happy to see him as well.

"Where's his bag and stuff?"

Shawn was used to Deena having him ready to go out the door. It had been months since he'd been in her apartment.

"It's ready. Can you come up for minute though? I need to talk to you about something."

He walked up the stairs and grabbed Aaron, throwing him up in the air. Aaron laughed.

"I missed you X-man. What you been up to?"

He held Aaron and walked in. Deena closed the door behind them.

"Daddy I got dis." Aaron held a tiny ball in his hand, showing it to Shawn.

Shawn focused on Deena. She went in her bedroom and came out with a folded piece of paper. She handed it to him and he put Aaron down and unfolded it.

"I got that in the mail the other day," she said.

It read:

Deena Marrell,

On behalf of St. Marshall Hospital, we have made several attempts to collect a debt from you in the amount of $3,596.00. Because we have not been contacted or received any payments in the amount owed, a judgment has been made against you and your employment wages will be garnished as of this date. To avoid further wage garnishment the payment should be made in full immediately.

Signed,
Seth Pozak
Attorney at Law

Deena was nervous. It was what she typed from her laptop that night she and Angie talked. She knew everyone had medical bills. And she knew Shawn couldn't question any hospital bills she had from Aaron's birth. They had never discussed it. She could make him believe she had a hospital bill she couldn't afford to pay. She found a colored logo from a law firm online and copied it onto the fake letter. The attorney she added on the letter was indicated as a partner at the law firm. She made a fake exaggerated signature of his name.

It looked like a real letter.

She tried to look relaxed. She had gone over the letter a hundred times since she wrote it.

"What's this for?" Shawn asked.

"A bill from his birth. My insurance paid everything but that's my part and I can't afford it."

She held out her hand for the letter and he gave it back to her. She didn't want him to look at it a second time.

"You haven't made *any* payments on it?"

"No. I can't," she said. "Look, I can't afford for them to garnish my wages because I won't be able to pay my rent."

Shawn didn't say anything.

"Daddy I go wit you?" Aaron stood in front of Shawn looking up at him.

He knew when Shawn came, the two of them left together and he was ready to go.

Shawn wasn't listening.

"Daddy I go wit you?" He said again.

He pulled on the bottom of Shawn's shirt to get his attention.

"Yeah, you're going with me. Hold on a minute."

Shawn looked at Deena.

"Can you give me the money to pay this?"

She held the tip of the letter out in her hand. She spoke again before he could.

"I know it's a lot of money and I would never ask you for this much, but I would literally lose my apartment if they garnish my wages," she said.

Shawn's face was serious. He was blindsided by the amount of money it was. He had never given her that much. He told her early on when Aaron was a baby that he understood if she went for child support but reassured her that she didn't have to. She knew she couldn't anyway. It was silent for too many seconds. She knew he was thinking about it.

"You don't want your son to be homeless, do you? Because you know he can't live with *you*."

She laid on the guilt. She didn't want him to say something like he'd give her half or just some of the money. She for sure couldn't afford for him to say no altogether. She didn't know how much longer she could avoid Toni seeing her sneak Aaron in and out of her apartment.

Aaron grew impatient. He pulled harder on Shawn's shirt.

"Daddy we go," he said pointing to the door.

"Okay, I'll get it to you when I drop him back off tomorrow night," Shawn said.

He didn't look at her. He picked up Aaron's bag and walked to the door. Aaron ran out and headed down the stairs holding the railing.

"Thank you so much," Deena said.

Shawn left and followed Aaron down the stairs.

"It's all good," he said without looking back at her.

CHAPTER 29

The move proved harder for Tia than anyone else. Angie found a place within blocks of the school and Tia no longer rode the school bus in the morning. She missed being with her friends on the bus singing songs and picking out different cars along the way pretending to claim them as their own. There weren't nearly as many cars on her two-block walk to and from school on side streets. The day care van still picked her up from school on days Angie worked, but there were only a few other kids on the ride with her. They were much younger and she had nothing in common with them.

She rarely saw Aaron at their daycare. Toddlers and babies were kept separate from older kids, so she only saw him when Angie picked them up in the evening. Aaron spent most of the day there since he wasn't school-age. Tia noticed another thing that changed with the new move. Aaron wasn't at home with them anymore. She remembered what Angie told her about Deena helping her out a lot with him and that he sometimes stayed with her. But he didn't come to the new place with them at all. Tia noticed that a lot of his clothes and bath toys were gone. Most of his favorite toys were gone too. Since she spent most weekends at her dad's house, she hardly knew Aaron was sometimes gone from home then too. But the weekdays were different. He wasn't around anymore to come in her room and twist the legs of her Barbies every which way. He couldn't grab her tubes of glitter from her art case and squirt them on the carpet. She didn't have to chase him around yelling for Angie to help her pry something from his hands that she caught him taking from her room. She still missed him. It wasn't the same at home without him. She figured he was with Deena all that time but didn't know why. Deena had never kept him that long. After a week, she asked Angie where he was.

"He's with the Deena for a while," she said hoping Tia would leave it at that.

"Why?" She asked.

Tia knew that much, but wanted to know the reason. There was still room for him at the new place. It was even bigger than the last one and she hadn't heard Angie complain about money lately, either.

"She's just keeping him a little while for something. He'll be back soon."

Angie was short with her. She had no other reason to give her eight-year-old who was old enough to be curious about her baby brother not being around. Angie couldn't lie to her in that moment. She hadn't thought of a good reason to give should Tia even ask.

"Is she going to bring him to my party?" Tia asked.

Her birthday was in a week and Angie promised her a party at a placed called Kid Zone Pizzeria. She invited some friends from school and her baby sister on her dad's side. She wanted Aaron to be there too of course.

"*Yes,* he will be at the party Tia. Why wouldn't he be?"

Angie stared at her in disbelief. Tia shrugged her shoulders. She didn't say anything.

"He's gonna for sure be at the party, okay?" Angie lowered her voice.

She couldn't be upset at her. It only made sense for Tia to think her brother may not make the party because he hadn't even been home with them. Angie was worried about what was going on in Tia's head about Deena having Aaron with her.

"Get ready so I can drop you off," she said to her.

Her mother was taking Tia early birthday shopping. She was going out of town in the next few days and wouldn't be able to see her on her actual birthday. She had grown close to her grandmother and was spending more time with her lately.

Tia put on her shoes and grabbed her purple overnight duffel bag. She was spending the night. Angie had to work and was meeting with a bride afterward about makeup for her wedding. Her mother wanted Tia to stay overnight. It worked out for Angie because her meetings always ran longer than she liked with someone not showing up on time or being overly picky on choices. She had a meeting one night until ten o'clock. Tia occupied Aaron for her, but they were both asleep on a chair by the time it was over. Angie felt bad having to drag them along and be out so late. It was almost a forty-minute drive to her mother's house from the new place. She only had enough time to watch Tia walk to the door to not be late for work. Her mother let Tia in and waved. She fanned her hand up and down signaling for Angie to let the car window down.

"Where's Aaron?" Her mother asked.

She didn't see him in the backseat. She also thought Angie would come inside for a little bit.

"Deena's keeping him for me," Angie yelled from the car. "I gotta work today."

"Oh, I didn't know you had to work," her mom yelled back. "You could've brought him too."

"No. Let Tia have her time with you. He's a handful. I'll see you tomorrow when you drop her off."

Angie drove away speeding to work. Her mother closed the door.

Tia put her duffel bag down and sat on the couch. Her grandmother had been watching a movie on TV. She handed Tia the remote control.

"You can watch something while I get ready," she said. "Why doesn't your mom ever bring Aaron over with you?"

She had only kept Aaron the one time when she took him and Tia Christmas shopping.

"He's always with Deena," Tia said.

"Why? She doesn't want *me* to keep him?"

"I think Deena wants to be his mom," Tia said with a sad look.

She told her grandmother about Aaron not moving to the new apartment with them and that most of his clothes and toys were gone.

"My mom just said he's staying with Deena for a little while and that Deena's helping her. But he's *always* with Deena so I think she wants to be his mom."

Her grandmother didn't go any further. She knew she couldn't say anything to Angie because she'd probably get upset at Tia for telling her. She couldn't help but wonder if Angie was struggling financially to keep up. The thought also crossed her mind that maybe Angie didn't want Aaron. She quickly dismissed those because she had seen how Angie was so overprotective of both of her kids and loved them more than life itself. She also realized Angie's finances weren't the issue because she just moved from a two bedroom to a three. She remembered someone seeing Aaron with her and saying they knew his dad. But his dad left and never came back according to Tia.

She was confused nonetheless. She didn't dwell on it too long and didn't want to get in Angie's private life. She got dressed and took Tia shopping.

———=•((•))•=———

Angie only got six RSVPs back from Tia's

classmates for the party. She prepared for the rest of the kids to just show up at the venue or their parents to call on the day of asking if they could still come.

She was right.

Two called before the party started and the rest just showed up. Tia's party room had been decorated with purple and teal balloons with plates, cups, and party favors to match. Angie had also drawn "BIRTHDAY GIRL" on Tia's cheek in purple and teal face paint. Tia grinned from ear to ear afterward. Angie was expecting Deena to bring Aaron and help her with the party since the parents were dropping the kids off and picking them up later.

Deena finally showed running twenty minutes late. She not only had Aaron but she brought Toni's daughter Jasmine. Aaron had spent time playing with her at Deena's. Deena let her come over sometimes and thought it would distract Aaron from going to the door saying, "I want my mama." She found that they played well together and Aaron liked having her around. She explained to Angie that she didn't plan on bringing Jasmine, but was keeping her for Toni until she was done at the salon. Toni called and told her the stylist overbooked clients and she would be another hour getting back. Deena had to bring Jasmine with her. She sent Jasmine and Aaron over to the toddler size bounce house. She and Angie watched them jump around inside. Jasmine's bushy ponytail bopped around on her head. Angie rolled her eyes.

"She does not need to see Aaron around me."

"She's four Angie," Deena said. "How could a four-year old possibly figure out what's going on with us?"

Deena walked around her and put their coats away. She opened paper plates and cups to set the party table for pizza. Angie walked over to keep an eye on Aaron and Jasmine.

Tia had a blast with her classmates. She kept a permanent grin on her face going from the different game stations and activities. She could be spotted anywhere at the party venue because Angie got her a huge shiny purple hair tie with curly ribbon streaming from it. It bounced around on her hair. She left her friends a few times to play with Aaron. She took him throughout the game area and lifted him up to reach the controllers on some of the games. Angie annoyed both of them, making them stop to take pictures together. Aaron especially got upset. It was too many things to do and see, and stopping to take pictures annoyed him.

"No pickas mama," he said to Angie.

She laughed.

"No pictures? Okay. No more pictures," she said.

She turned her camera off and left it hanging around her neck. The party went well and the kids had fun. Tia had a good time and got so many gifts Angie's backseat and trunk were filled with them when it was time to leave. Tia's dad Brian had come and brought the biggest gift she got. It was a bigger TV for her room and the main thing she wanted. He said her little sister was sick and couldn't make it. Tia was okay with that. She saw her most weekends. She was mostly happy Aaron was there and she got to spend time with him. It was her best birthday.

CHAPTER 30

Entrepreneurship had been paying off for Angie. Her services had extended from weddings to women celebrating birthdays, retirements, and anniversaries. She made a photo album to show her work and women loved a photo of a four-generation family. They were all dressed in a pink champagne color with a gray backdrop. Angie had done their makeup for the photos. It was a big hit when people paged through her album and saw it.

One request she never thought she'd get was to do the makeup of a dead woman at a funeral home. It was left on her voicemail. She was sickened at the idea but sort of flattered that someone felt she was the person to make their loved one look good. Why wasn't the funeral home staff good enough? She struggled with returning the call and saying no. She reached out to her mom for advice. Makeup was the one thing the two of them had in common.

"Whoa," her mom said. "That's unusual."

"I'm weirded out by it and I don't think I can do something like that," Angie said, scrunching her face while holding the phone to her ear.

Her mother reassured her that the woman was not

going to raise up from the casket and get her. They both laughed. She told her that hairstylists get asked all the time to do hair for funerals. Angie was still grossed out but listened.

"Why don't you call the family member back and ask a few questions? I'm sure you'll find out why they don't want the funeral home to do it."

"Yeah, and I can always say no but it won't keep me from feeling bad about it," Angie said.

She returned the call the next day and found out that the woman was forty-seven years old and died of a sudden brain aneurism. Her sister told Angie that she had always done her own makeup exceptionally well. She prided herself on it and always looked beautiful. It was why they wanted Angie to do it and not the funeral home staff.

She mustered up the strength and accepted the job. She felt sad for the woman who died too young and unexpectedly. When the day came, she took her mother's advice and pretended the woman was a manikin just to get through it. The family had given her a picture of the woman and she saw that her makeup *was* flawless. She used similar colors as to what she saw in the picture and got through it. She was creeped out by being in an eerie funeral home and she hoped it was her first and only request like that ever.

The mall kiosk lasted longer than most, but the owner's sales were down and she had to cut Angie's hours and run the kiosk herself mostly. She couldn't offer makeup sessions anymore and just relied on sales. Angie started working part of the day with her to help out. She hadn't told her she was already looking for a different job and was tired of working at the kiosk anyway. A new makeup store called Face had just opened near the mall. Angie applied as one of the two cosmeticians needed. It was the job she was looking for. She got the call to start the following week after interviewing. She was excited to land a better job and it was a full-time position.

She loaned her car to Kayla again the day before she started. Kayla told her Derrick needed their car for another out-of-town trip. Angie was at home all day that Sunday, and Monday was her big day. She hadn't heard from Kayla since she got the car the day before, but Kayla knew what time to bring the car back so she could start work at 10AM when the store opened. She did her makeup after getting dressed and by then it was nine o'clock. Kayla was supposed to be pulling up outside a few minutes later, but was calling instead.

"You on your way?" Angie asked as soon as she answered.

"No. Is it a way you can get a cab to work for today?" Kayla said sounding upset.

"Why?! Where's my car?" Angie yelled.

"Don't get upset. Derrick has it."

Angie panicked. It was after nine and she had to start in less than an hour. It took at least twenty minutes to get there.

"What do you mean Derrick has it? Why the

hell does he have my car and where is he?" Angie screamed.

"He used it to give somebody a ride out of town. He won't make it back today."

"What?!"

Angie was almost in tears. Nothing Kayla said made sense to her and she didn't believe her.

"Where are you?!" Angie yelled.

Kayla had driven to where Derrick was supposed to be, but his phone was dead. She found out he had driven even further away to do what he was doing. She planned on getting Angie's car and switching with him. She was going to try to make it back in time, but was still too far away. She had to tell Angie.

"What the fuck is he doing with my car?!"

Angie started to cry a little. She was overwhelmed.

"Angie, call a cab so you don't miss work," Kayla pleaded with her.

Guilt was in her voice.

"Or I'm gonna hang up and call one for you. You can still make it to work."

Angie hung up. Tears welled in her eyes. She called a cab and made it to her new job ten minutes late. She had called the manager quickly before leaving home. She said her car was being serviced at the dealership and it took longer than she thought so she had to get a ride. It worked but she was still embarrassed and mad as hell.

On her forty-five-minute lunch break at two o'clock, she called the police to report the car stolen.

She had two missed calls from Kayla that morning. She only called Kayla back quickly to be told Derrick still wasn't back yet. She didn't tell Kayla she reported her car stolen. She didn't care if Derrick was actually on his way back with it. He had no business driving it and she came to the realization that he may not have had the car at all anymore. Why wasn't he back yet? What was he doing? Why did he have her car in the first place instead of their car? She was confused. She told the police officer it was stolen from a family member after she let her borrow it. She felt better knowing that whatever illegal thing her car was being used for, she wouldn't be held responsible.

The police officer was finally done taking the report and drove away. Angie had missed all but five minutes of her lunch break. She had just enough time to run across the big busy street to a small convenient store and grab a bag of snack crackers to eat. She shoved them on a shelf inside one of the makeup counters and sneaked them little by little while she worked. It was enough to keep her stomach from growling too loud in front of customers. She put her game face on and kept working. She was supposed to familiarize herself with the Face brand and colors she didn't know if there was downtime. It was none of that. The store was busy from the time she started. She hadn't checked her phone at all. It was seven o'clock and time for the store to close. She picked it up to call a cab home. She had two more missed calls from Kayla and one from the police department. She called the police department back first of course. It was about her car.

It was found and towed and the driver was arrested. Angie gasped out loud. She called back. Derrick had been arrested driving the car. He had been pulled over for speeding and a check of the license plate showed the car was stolen. The officer asked her if she knew Derrick. She told him he was her cousin's boyfriend and had no permission to drive her car. She tried to talk quickly. She was in a back "employee only" room. People were coming to get their things to leave. The manager had locked the front door to close the store for the day. Angie had said her car was being serviced. She didn't want people to hear her answer questions about it being stolen. There was nowhere else to go in the store to talk privately. She hadn't even called a cab yet. She only had a few more minutes before she was the last one there. Two more people came in laughing and talking.

"Can I talk to you when I get home? She quietly asked the officer. "I'm off work now and have to call a cab before it's too late."

The officer met Angie at her apartment. He was parked there when the cab pulled up. He needed to talk with her further in person. She let him inside and found herself being interrogated. Stolen electronics were found in her car when Derrick was arrested. They had been stolen from a large store about thirty miles from where he was stopped and the police learned they had been taken by a store employee who was friends with him. Derrick had been travel-ing to the area transporting the property back to sell it to various people he knew. He'd buy it all from his friend for a few hundred dollars and sell it for much more. Angie figured it had to be why he needed her car sometimes. It was much bigger to load more stuff. Kayla's new car was too small.

Angie convinced the officer that she was not in-volved in anything Derrick did and she didn't know he used her car to do it. She was fuming so much she didn't hear much of what the officer said before he left. It was something about where and when to pick her car up. She dug down in her purse for her phone and was about to call Kayla. Her phone rang before she could dial and it was her. She was already screaming before Angie could.

"Why'd you say the car was stolen?! Derrick got arrested!"

"Don't call me with that!" Angie yelled right back. "You lied every time you borrowed my car!"

"He didn't use your car every time I borrowed it and I always brought it back to you!" Kayla screamed over Angie trying to talk. "And I asked you not to re-port it stolen because he was coming back with it!"

It was what Kayla asked in her voicemail to Angie. Angie had never heard Kayla sound that way. She was more in a rage than her. Angie couldn't out-scream her so she stopped and held the phone. Kayla yelled about Derrick being only a half-hour away and would've just gotten a speeding ticket had she not reported the car stolen. Angie got a pause and jumped in.

"I'm not gonna press charges about the car so he's gotta deal with the other issue of having stolen property. That's on him," she said.

"Okay, but it's your fault for reporting the car stolen when you know it wasn't stolen! That's alright. Karma is a bitch!" Kayla said and hung up.

Angie threw her phone on the couch and plopped down. She was so worked up she had to calm herself down and take a deep breath. How could Kayla be okay with her boyfriend doing something like that? And letting him use *her* car to do it? She put her face in her hands and cried.

CHAPTER 31

"Come here Xavier!" Deena called out to Aaron from her bedroom.

He had been playing with Jasmine most days whenever he and Deena were home. She usually let Jasmine come down the hall to her apartment. Aaron would ask for her. It seemed to keep him from asking for Angie. She had let him go to Toni's apartment to play with Jasmine but it was only on a few short occasions. She felt uneasy about it with Aaron starting to talk much better. She didn't want Toni asking him things and figuring stuff out.

"Xavier!" Deena yelled for him again.

She could hear Jasmine trying to get a toy from him, telling him it was her turn. She heard Jasmine say something else, but couldn't quite make out what it was. Aaron came to the bedroom.

"Didn't I tell you to share?"

Deena sat up in the bed and paused the movie she was watching. Aaron stood in the doorway and stayed quiet.

"You hear what I said?"

He shook his head yes. He started back for the living room and Deena called him back to her.

"I heh you," he said.

"Wait right there."

Deena called Jasmine to the room and she came and stood next to Aaron.

"What toy is he not sharing with you? The one in his hand?"

"Yeah," Jasmine said with a sad look. "We take turns driving it on the floor and he keeps taking a long time to let me do it," she said.

She looked at Aaron while she said it.

"What else were you saying to him?" Deena asked.

She knew she heard Jasmine lower her voice and say something else to Aaron because he wouldn't give her the toy. Jasmine looked right at her and didn't hesitate.

"I told him I was gonna tell his mama because I know who his real mama is."

Deena felt like she was punched in the stomach.

She swung her legs over and sat on the side of the bed. She had to talk to her fast. It was the only thing she could do to convince her.

"A..Xavier go play with your truck. Let me talk to Jasmine for a minute," Deena said.

She was so worked up she almost made the slip and called him Aaron. He ran back to the living room and Deena heard him put the truck down and start moving it around the floor. She had Jasmine come over to her by the bed.

"Jasmine. I *am* his mama, okay?"

Jasmine stayed quiet.

"Why would you think I'm not?"

"I saw his mama at the birthday party. Your friend. He was calling *her* mama," Jasmine said.

Deena was stumped for a second. Angie warned her this would happen. She did underestimate a four-year old.

Jasmine stood staring at her with wide puppy-like eyes as if she said something wrong.

"Listen," Deena said. "That's my friend and sometimes he calls her mama."

Deena knew she couldn't say Jasmine misheard what Aaron was saying that day. All she could do was convince her that what she thought was true was not.

"When he was a baby, he lived with her for a while because I moved away. So, he started calling her mama because I wasn't around and he still calls her that sometimes."

Jasmine shook her head yes like she understood. She held the puppy dog stare at Deena.

"It's okay. You didn't know, but now you do."

Jasmine shook her head again without saying anything.

"You can go back and play," Deena said.

Jasmine walked back to the living room. Deena yelled to Aaron for him to share his toys and take turns with her.

"Damn Angie was right," she said to herself.

She forgot how Tia soaked up things like a sponge at that age. Angie couldn't talk around her because she'd repeat to her dad what anyone said. And it was almost word for word. Deena just thought she was a smarter-than-usual four-year old. Now seeing Jasmine put two and two together, they all seemed to be little sponges.

Deena hoped she was convincing enough. Jasmine couldn't be that smart but Deena wasn't sure if she had told Toni. Toni hadn't said anything but was she watching closely now and keeping it to herself? Deena knew her like a book. She would've said something about it right away. Her curiosity always got the best of her.

Deena called Angie. She didn't need Jasmine hearing the conversation so she turned the TV volume up in the living room and went back and closed her bedroom door.

"You were right," Deena said as soon as she answered.

"Right about what? What happened?"

"About Jasmine. She told me she knows that you're Aaron's real mama."

She spoke low.

"What?!"

"Yes. She heard him calling you that at the party," Deena said almost in a whisper.

"See I told you. I would've rather you just came late with him and dropped her off first."

"I know."

Deena rolled her eyes.

"Did Toni say somethin'?"

"Nope. She would've by now, knowing her. I told

Jasmine he lived with you for a while when he was a baby and he started calling you mama."

Deena cracked her bedroom door open to make sure Jasmine wasn't standing by listening.

"I am literally in my closed bedroom hiding from a child so she can't hear what I'm saying," Deena said still speaking low.

"I told you these kids are smart," Angie said.

She reminded Deena of how smart Tia was at four.

"We need to worry about Aaron now and what may come out of his mouth soon."

"Yeah." Deena sighed.

"Well, you were right about something too," Angie said. "Kayla borrowing my car."

She sounded defeated.

"What happened?"

"Derrick was using it to bring back stolen stuff from a guy he knows doing employee thefts at a store."

Angie told her all about how Derrick got arrested and she and Kayla were no longer on speaking terms.

"Why?"

"I reported my car stolen when she told me he had it and he got pulled over in it. The police searched the car and found the stolen stuff. She's mad saying he would've just gotten a speeding ticket if I wouldn't have reported the car stolen."

"Wow, she's got some nerve getting mad at you when she lied to you about the car in the first place!"

Deena caught herself getting louder and went and peeked out her door again. Aaron and Jasmine were still in the living room. He was putting one of his toy men in his remote-control truck. Jasmine was fixated on a cartoon on TV. Deena closed her door back.

Angie told her how Kayla didn't seem to get that point and hung up on her.

"I don't care about her being mad. I'm just as mad as she is."

"Wait." Deena thought about it. "How mad is she? Remember she knows about us?"

Angie hesitated.

"Well, that's what I was gonna tell you. She said 'karma's a bitch' before she hung up on me."

"Mmmmmmhh!" Deena screamed with her mouth closed. "Angie! She probably told some people already and it's just a matter of time before it gets back to Shawn!"

"Calm down," Angie said.

Deena brought up the wedding and how it would be nothing for Kayla to call up her friend who'd tell her husband. Angie told her that Kayla was friends with the girl who got married and she was asked at the last minute to be in the wedding after somebody dropped out, but they weren't that close.

"And that girl's husband isn't friends with Shawn. They just go to the same barber," Angie said, as if she was reassuring herself.

"So! I don't put anything past her," Deena said.

"She'll figure out how to make it known. I can see her making calls now."

"All those girls in the wedding know I'm his mom anyway. They saw him there with me. I think it'll take some work on her part to get people to believe that."

"I'm scared now." Deena paced back and forth in her room. "Why didn't you tell me this yesterday?"

"Because I knew you'd be like you are now *and* I don't think she'll do that."

Angie reminded Deena that Kayla hadn't even asked about their situation with Aaron in a long time. She didn't even know Aaron was living with Deena.

"She would more than love to pay you back by getting at me," Deena said. "That's what she meant by karma's a bitch. I'll pay you back by fucking your friend over."

Angie was at work on a break. It was time to go back out to the floor.

"We'll talk about it when you bring Aaron home tonight."

It was the weekend and she was off work Sunday. Aaron would be there with her for the next couple of days.

"Okay," Deena said angrily.

She had been in her favorite soft blue pajamas all day. The second movie she was on was paused in the middle since she talked to Jasmine. Watching movies was her plan for the day. Now she was scared and couldn't relax. She worried about where Kayla was in the process of dropping the bomb on her. She thought of Shawn calling her and cursing her at the top of his lungs. Or being at the door as soon as she opened it, grabbing her by the throat and choking her to death without saying a word. It was already a scene she played over and over in her head. Now it seemed like it would really happen.

She panicked.

What if he knew? What if he was standing at the door when she left? She could see the rage in his eyes.

Aaron banging something in the living room snapped her out of it. She looked around the room. Her pint of chocolate ice cream she had been eating was melting. She grabbed it and put it in the freezer and Jasmine was on a stepstool at the sink getting some water. Deena suddenly remembered her talk with her. It was all caving in around her. She couldn't dismiss the fact that Jasmine may mention something to Toni. She could see that too. Toni would ask her about it. She'd deny it and Toni would start doing her digging to figure it out. It would somehow get back to Shawn and things would end the same way. He would be standing at the door with rage. Jasmine got down from the stepstool and drank her water. Deena waited until she was done.

"You remember what we talked about Jasmine?"

Jasmine shook her head yes.

"What did I say?"

Jasmine put her cup down without looking at her.

"That you Es-say-veeas real mama."

She started heading off to the living room.

"Okay," Deena said.

She hoped their conversation stayed there in the apartment. She couldn't be sure it would.

"Xavier come on and get dressed. We gotta go." Deena called into the living room for Aaron.

She was in a hurry all of a sudden to get out of the apartment. She didn't know what Kayla was working up and didn't want to be caught at home. The scene with Shawn wouldn't leave her mind. She walked into the living room.

"Jasmine come on. I'll walk you back down the hall to your mom. We're about to leave."

She walked Jasmine to Toni's door and when Toni closed her door back, Deena speeded Aaron down the hall to hurry and get dressed. The phone rang and it was her grandmother.

That was where she'd go with Aaron.

Shawn never knew where she lived. She'd stay there with him until Angie got off work.

"Hey grandma. I was just about to come over there and check on you. You home?"

Deena packed up Aaron's things as she talked.

"Yeah. I was calling to see if you could bring me some eggs from the store," she said.

She told Deena she promised a friend she'd make a cake for the church bake sale and forgot to get eggs when she went grocery shopping.

"Yeah, you can have mine. I'll be heading that way now."

She was in the middle of putting Aaron on his jacket.

"I'm watching Angie's son until she gets off work. Do you remember me telling you about him?" Deena asked, holding the phone with one ear pressed against her shoulder.

She had told her grandmother when Aaron was born that Angie had another baby, but it would be the first time her grandmother saw him.

"He's almost three years old now," Deena said.

She grabbed her carton of eggs from the fridge and hurried out the door.

CHAPTER 32

Deena stayed at Angie's apartment for the next two nights and went back home on Monday morning to get ready for work. She wanted Aaron to be home with Angie for the week. Nothing would've been worse if he was caught in the drama of Shawn showing up to confront her. She picked him up at day care and met Angie at her apartment. She knew nosy Toni would ask about him eventually. She told her she had to work late hours for the week so he was staying with his grandmother on his dad's side. Even though she went back, she purposely stayed away from home after work until late in the night for the next few days. If Shawn came by, he would see her car parked in the back and know she was home. She was safe after it got late enough. A married man certainly wouldn't be prowling around too late no matter the reason. The later it got she avoided Toni too. She was coming home well after eleven o'clock and knew Toni was in bed by then.

The building was always quiet. Deena had only come home that late one time since she lived there. She could hear the TV playing in apartment seven, right at the back door. There was no one moving around at least that she could hear, except herself. She felt as if she was disturbing everyone with the heavy back door that always slammed loudly when it closed. This mission to avoid Shawn was already getting old. She hadn't heard from him about anything, and the chance of coming home late and getting assaulted or robbed was more likely to happen than running into him.

The week played out well with no surprises and it was Shawn's weekend with Aaron. He usually called to pick him up by 10AM. Deena headed over to Angie's to wait. She was still nervous about Aaron being with him if the truth came out. Angie admitted that she didn't know where Kayla was in the scheme of things but kept replaying her "karma's a bitch" comment over and over in her head.

"I still think she would've done it by now," she said.

They talked low so Tia wouldn't hear them. She was still asleep in her bedroom. Angie found out Kayla had bailed Derrick out of jail sometime during the week.

Deena was even more nervous.

"I just don't trust her," she said. "She still may be trying to get her friends from the wedding to put her in touch with him."

Since Shawn got Aaron every other weekend, she felt better waiting for two more weeks to go by. A half a day with him was better than the whole weekend.

"I'll tell him I got a cousin in town and she's

leaving tomorrow evening so we're gonna hang out with her," Deena said, staring into space concentrating on her quick plan.

"So, you don't want him to go with him this weekend?" Angie asked.

"Yes. He can. But it'll just be for half the day and I'll tell him he needs to be back home."

Deena got out her cell phone.

"And I'm actually gonna call him first so it won't sound like I waited until he was on his way to get him."

"Go in the hallway and call," Angie whispered to her.

She reminded her about Tia in the bedroom.

"I don't want her to hear you saying Xavier."

Deena stepped out to the hallway and dialed Shawn's number. She calmed herself and tried to sound normal.

"I was just about to call you," he said.

Deena could hear that he was getting in his car.

"Do you mind bringing him to the transport office? One of my drivers didn't show up and I gotta drive in his place today."

She had worried for a split second about what he would say.

"Wheew!" Deena whispered to herself, pushing the phone out from her face and dropping her head down to her knees in relief.

"Okay what time?"

She quickly gathered herself and stood up straight.

"Now if you can. My mother will watch him until I finish these three pick-ups."

Deena had to tell him Aaron couldn't stay the whole weekend.

"Oh yeah that's what I wanted to tell you. My cousin is in town and she wants to see Xavier. She's leaving tomorrow and it's our only day to hang out with her. I need to pick him up at least by three."

"Oh." Shawn paused. "Well since my weekend is cut short, am I taking next weekend then?"

Deena thought for a second. If things didn't blow up in their face by then, it would probably be okay.

She still hesitated.

"Okay. Yeah," she said.

"Well I would say we could skip today but my mother wanted to see him," he said. "Just meet me at the office with him and she'll come and get him from me."

Deena had never met Shawn's mother in person. She had only talked to her a couple of times over the phone about Aaron's medication when she kept him and he was sick. Shawn kept the two of them from meeting. Deena wasn't sure if his mother wanted it that way or if he did. She knew it was probably best that way. The less anyone saw her, the better.

She went back inside Angie's apartment.

"Nothing yet," she said, as if the coast was clear.

Angie put her finger up to her lips to keep Deena to a whisper from Tia.

"Okay so what time is he getting picked up?" Angie asked.

"At three. But I'm dropping him off at the transport office and I gotta pick him up from there too. His mother is gonna keep him since he's gotta drive for somebody."

"Aaron give me a kiss. You gotta go with Deena," Angie said.

He walked over to her and kissed her cheek.

"You'll be back later okay?"

Aaron shook his head yes. He followed Deena out the door.

"You're going to see your daddy," Deena said to him.

"Daddy pick me up?" He asked.

Aaron knew he was always picked up by Shawn.

"No. I'm taking you to him. I'll pick you up later."

She called Shawn when she got there. There were six transport vans parked in the lot on an angle against the building. JC TRANSPORT was the name of the business. It was painted in brown cursive letters on the side of each van. Shawn's uncle's name was John Carter. He had been with the transport business for the elderly more than twenty years. Deena parked in an empty space between two of the vans. She headed to the front door and Shawn met her. He picked Aaron up and tossed him in the air, catching him. Aaron laughed.

"What's up my man?" Shawn said to him.

"C'mon. I'll take you for a quick ride in one of the vans before your grandma gets here."

Shawn took him by the hand and headed inside. He told Deena to meet him back there at three o'clock.

———————⟫⟨◉⟩⟪———————

Angie stayed in Saturday evening with Tia and Aaron. Deena dropped him off at around 3:45 that afternoon and he had fallen asleep in the car. He wasted no time going back to sleep on the living room couch. Shawn told Deena his kids were at his mom's house and they wore Aaron out running around in the backyard all day. Angie could tell he had been outside. She picked a few blades of grass out of his hair and let him sleep. Tia was happy he slept. Angie promised to watch a movie with her and they were just getting started. She always liked to see Angie pop popcorn in a pot on the stove the old-fashioned way. It was Angie's favorite. She hated microwave popcorn and didn't have a popcorn popper. Tia stood back and grinned with wide eyes at the popcorn hitting the pot cover. Angie filled them some bowls and started the movie. Aaron stayed asleep.

Her phone rang about ten minutes into the movie. It was the number to Face, the makeup store. She paused the movie and answered it. It was her supervisor asking if she could work the next day. She had been given the weekend off surprisingly after just starting the job.

"Umm." She hesitated.

She had worked open to close all week and wanted her two days off in a row with her kids.

"I know you worked long hours all week," her supervisor said. "We'll pay you time and a half."

She reminded Angie that Sunday's hours for her would only be from two to five.

"We don't have a makeup specialist for tomorrow. You're the only one and we screwed up the schedule."

Face was still trying to find a second makeup specialist since the store opened. Angie didn't want to say no. It was a new job and one she was really happy to get. Time and half pay sounded good too.

"Okay, I can come in."

Tia stared at her with one hand in her popcorn. Angie hung up the phone.

"Yeah I know," she said to her.

She promised she'd do something with her the next day after work.

"I don't think your grandmother is busy tomorrow. I'll see if she can watch you and Aaron for me. And then we'll go out to eat when I get off."

Tia was happy. She'd get to pick the restaurant. Angie started the movie up again and they munched popcorn and giggled while Aaron slept.

Angie rushed the kids to her mother's the next day and headed to work. She got busy around three

o'clock with two hours until close. She had just
finished doing makeup for a woman trying a new
foundation. She was cleaning up the station and sent
the woman to the front of the store to check out. A
customer had come to the back and was looking at
eyeshadows. She started testing them on the backs
of her hand. Angie noticed she had looked over at
her a couple of times while she straightened up her
makeup station. She wiped the chair down with a
clean towel and walked over to the girl.

"Can I help you find something?" She asked.

The girl looked up at her.

"No, I'm good," she said.

She seemed serious and just kept studying the
two eyeshadow colors on her hands, putting them
side-by-side. Angie took the opportunity to tell her
about the sale on certain brands.

"Well just so you know, the Margot and Leeza
brands are twenty percent off today."

Angie pointed to them. The girl rolled her eyes.

"And just so you know, it's not cool to mess
around with peoples' husbands," she said. And it's
even worse having a baby by one."

Angie frowned and couldn't believe what she
said. The girl knew about Deena and Shawn and had
her mistaken with Deena. Angie didn't back down
but kept her cool because she was at work.

"You don't even know me so I advise you to
mind your business," she said.

She rolled her eyes and walked away from the

girl. Another employee was walking toward the back. She didn't see the exchange between them and asked the girl if she needed help with something.

"No. I found what I was looking for but I'll buy it somewhere else," the girl said.

She turned and walked out the store leaving the eyeshadow tester drawers open. Angie watched her leave and didn't say anything about what happened.

Who *was* that bitch? It was all Angie could think as she stared at the door long after the girl left. She felt the word *BITCH* trying to force itself through her closed mouth. She wanted to scream it at her. She wanted to run outside, grab her by the hair, and bang her head into a car in the parking lot. She'd learn not to get in other folks' business.

She walked in the employee room. It was 4:30. She didn't plan on going back out to the floor. Usually the last-minute rush-ins knew exactly what they wanted and bought it and left. She waited out her last few minutes and called Deena on her way to the car. She made it just in time because it started to rain.

"Some bitch just came in Face and said I shouldn't be having babies by a married man," she said.

"Who was that?!" Deena asked.

"I have no idea. Most likely somebody from the wedding who saw me with Aaron."

They both figured that was the case. Shawn had told some of the guys at the barbershop he had another son. Angie remembered there were a few women at the wedding that had peeked into the ladies' lounge looking for certain bridesmaids. They saw her with Aaron and could've assumed she hooked up with Shawn and got pregnant with him. Angie drove to her mother's house to get Aaron and Tia.

It rained harder.

"Or it could be too that they may have seen Aaron out with him in public and remembered him from the wedding," Deena said.

"But that was over a year ago!" Angie said.

She thought it was ridiculous that a person would remember a baby over an adult.

"His looks haven't changed much. He's just a little bigger," Deena said. "Besides, you don't know when that person could've seen them together. It could've been around that time and now she sees you again and decided to say somethin."

Angie didn't say anything. She focused on the street, frustrated at the situation and the rain didn't help. Her wipers were at full speed beating across the windshield. Deena wrecked her brain to think of who the girl was and how she knew.

"Kayla was there. Do you think she said somethin?" Deena asked.

"But why would she tell anybody that *I* was the one with Shawn?"

Angie didn't think it made any sense.

"I don't put it past her to do that," Deena said. "Remember, she's pissed at you so she could make people think that to try to make you look bad."

"You don't know Kayla like I do. That would not give her enough satisfaction. What we're doing is worse than just making me look bad."

Angie had her cell phone on speaker on her lap. She gripped the steering wheel and leaned forward to see through the downpour. Her windshield wipers on full blast weren't standing up to the rain. She was too upset and didn't want to talk anymore.

"Let me get through this rain," she said. "I'll call you later."

CHAPTER 33

Mondays always felt like Mondays. Alarm clocks seemed to blare louder after the weekend was over. Deena pounded the snooze on hers and put her head under the covers. In ten more minutes, it wouldn't have been as loud with her head buried. It was Monday. It was just as loud as the first time. She had slept an hour longer because Aaron was staying with Angie for another week. She didn't have to get him ready or drive him to day care. It was still gloomy out from the rain the day before. Sun coming through the windows would've helped her get up faster, but after two snoozes she finally did. She had to hit the freeway early on Mondays to get to work on time.

It was 7:25 AM. It rained so hard overnight, huge puddles had formed around some of the cars in the parking lot. Deena needed to get to the freeway by 7:30. She stepped lightly across the puddles to get to her car and avoid splashing water up on her gray dress slacks. She pressed her arm tight against her purse and held her pant legs up. It was no use because her car and the one next to it sat in what looked like a mini flood in the parking lot. She swore her next apartment would come with indoor parking. She had wasted five minutes already just to get to her car and avoid puddles only to step in one anyway and get soaked. She let go of her pant legs and grabbed her car door to get in. Her feet were soaked and the bottom of her pants dripped around them. She reversed her car out of the water and headed out to the busy Monday traffic. It was 7:31 AM and it was stop and go on the entrance ramp at the freeway.

Her phone rang. She reached inside her purse over on the seat with one hand, keeping her eyes ahead. It was Shawn. It had to be that he wanted to get Aaron the upcoming weekend since his got cut short.

"Hello," she said loudly.

She had sat the phone on the front seat and put it on speaker.

"You on your way to work?" He asked.

"Yeah."

"Where's Xavier? Or should I say *Aaron*?"

Deena swallowed and coughed like she choked. He knew.

She stayed in the right lane and still had four exits to pass before she got to hers. She gripped the steering wheel.

"Huh?!"

It was all she could say. Her chest felt tight and she sped up without realizing it. Shawn went on.

"Huh?! That's all you got?! Yeah, I know about *Aaron.* I found out after you picked him up from me Saturday." Shawn had a weird, calm rage in his voice. "So, I just couldn't sit back and let you get away with it. Did you think it would just be a phone call and I curse you out and we part ways?"

Deena squeezed the steering wheel.

"Don't hurt that baby! Let me explain everything to you. It wasn't meant to go that way," she pleaded.

"I would never hurt *any* child and bitch you can't explain shit to me!" He screamed. "I'm the wrong person to fuck with! We'll see if you make it to work!"

Deena only made out part of what he said next. She saw her exit coming up. A small red car cut in front of her and she stepped on the brakes to avoid hitting it. Her brake pedal pressed to the floor and she couldn't stop. The brakes had gone out. She screamed and swerved the car. Her purse and cell phone slammed to the floor. She flipped over off the side of the road. Her car went down the small grassy hill and her airbags looked like white pillows bursting through the windows. Her car flipped again, smashing the roof in until it came to rest on its side with the driver's door facing the sky. Smoke billowed out of the car's back end. Freeway drivers had stopped in the emergency lane and looked over the side. Deena was unconscious and pulled from the car by firefighters who got there after a few minutes. She was rushed to the hospital.

Doctors surrounded her in the trauma room and worked to get her breathing better. A big oxygen mask covered most of her face. An IV was put in her right hand and a doctor dabbed an open gash on her forehead that had been dumping out blood when she was pulled from the car. It was stitched right away by a nurse who was off to the side prepping the materials for it. She pulled the gash together, sticking a needle into Deena's skin on both sides to close it. Deena didn't move. She was still unconscious.

———⟫(◍)⟪———

Angie was given the day off in place of working on Sunday. She was going through her fridge and cabinets making her grocery list to head to the store. Aaron watched cartoons in the living room and she speeded over to the TV to turn it down. Her phone was ringing.

It was Deena's grandmother. She told her she got a call from the hospital and that Deena had been in a bad car accident. Angie almost dropped the phone. Deena's grandmother knew they were close and Deena would want Angie there.

"My son is on his way to get me and we're gonna rush there," she said.

"Yes ma'am. I'm leaving right now. I'll see you there."

Angie hung up the phone and called her mother to keep Aaron. She hung up on the second ring. The daycare was much closer than her mother's and she could get to the hospital faster. She dropped him off and headed there. Deena's grandmother wasn't given any information on her condition. She told Angie they only said Deena was in a bad car accident and they needed next of kin to consent to sign for surgery. Angie could only think it had to be pretty bad if that was the case.

She kept trying to picture the accident. Was she hit or did she hit someone? It ran through Angie's head. She fought back tears knowing Deena always wore her seatbelt and was a pretty safe driver.

She made it to the hospital and ran inside from the parking structure. Deena had been admitted to the intensive care unit. Angie knew it was serious. The double doors to the unit swung open and she was allowed inside. She had to give her name and there were only two visitors per patient. She was directed to room nine. It was the same room number she had in the labor and delivery unit at Mercy Hospital after she gave birth to Aaron. The hallway was low-lit and eerily quiet. The nurses walking around were soft-ly talking to each other in almost a whisper. Room nine was only four rooms down the hall from the en-trance, but Angie felt like she was walking a mile in slow motion.

She stopped at the room and peeked in. She was the first one there. Deena's grandmother and uncle hadn't made it yet. She walked into the room and saw her friend lying there. Her eyes were closed in sleep or unconsciousness. Angie wasn't sure.

The room was quiet and dark like the hallway other than annoying beeping coming from the machines hooked up to her. Angie stood quiet at the bed staring at her. She wiped her tears away to be strong. She always thought it was bad to let a person in that condition see or feel others cry. It weakened them even more.

"Deena," Angie said softly.

She leaned over to see if she could hear her.

"Deena," she said a little louder and put her hand on hers.

Deena opened her eyes. Angie was relieved that it was just a deep sleep. Her head was wrapped in thick gauze. Her left leg was in a sling and an oxygen mask covered her mouth and nose.

"Hey I'm here. Your grandmother and uncle are on their way."

Deena just looked at her. Her mouth moved under the oxygen mask. Angie lightly lifted it and leaned over to hear her better.

"It was Shawn. He knows."

Deena's voice was raspy and she hardly got it out.

Angie felt like she had to vomit. She scanned the room quickly to find the trash can but held it in. Her hands shook.

"How? What did he do?!"

Angie had so many questions. She tried to keep her voice low. She lifted Deena's mask again to hear her reply.

"He told me he knew about Aaron and he did something to my brakes."

Angie barely heard her but made out *brakes* and *Aaron*.

"I barely heard you," Angie said a little louder. "What happened with your brakes and who told him about Aaron?"

She was desperate to know. Deena's eyes closed and she didn't answer.

"Deena! Deena!" Angie said loudly.

She didn't respond or open her eyes again. The nurse came in making her usual rounds.

"She's in and out of consciousness," the nurse said.

She walked over to one of the machines and pressed the buttons to check numbers. Angie had no idea what she was monitoring. Her emotions were all over the place. She stared at Deena hoping she would wake up.

"She woke up and was talking to me," Angie said to the nurse without looking at her.

"Oh. Well it probably took a lot out of her just to say whatever she said. She has no energy but we're monitoring her blood pressure and other things."

The nurse checked Deena's pulse and fixed some of the cords coming from the machines.

"Sleep is good for her right now," she said.

The nurse walked out and said she'd be checking back in another half-hour or so. Angie was devastated inside. She stared at Deena sleeping. She was sad and frustrated. Did Shawn do something to her brakes after he found out about Aaron? Is that what Deena was trying to tell her? She cried hard. She couldn't hold back her tears anymore, but she turned away from Deena to cry. She was hot inside and felt sick. She wanted her friend to wake up and get better. She sat down in a chair across the room and put her head in her hands. Her mind went back to Shawn. Who told him about Aaron? Did he cause Deena's accident or was she so upset over him knowing about Aaron that she couldn't press her brakes fast enough and crashed?

Angie couldn't figure it out. She stared at the floor going over Deena's words in her head. Deena's grandmother and uncle came in. A different nurse had walked into the room and asked Angie to leave. It was the *two visitors only* policy for the ICU. Angie hugged them and they asked her if she knew what happened.

"No. She said a few words that I could barely make out and then fell back to sleep."

It was all Angie could say. She couldn't tell anybody that Deena's accident probably had something to do with her son and Deena's hard fall for a married man. She said goodbye to satisfy the drill sergeant nurse standing there, and reassured Deena's grandmother that she'd be back the next day and every day until Deena got better. Her eyes were bloodshot red from crying. She headed to her car almost running and couldn't get Deena's words '*It was Shawn. He knows*' out of her head. It dawned on her that Deena found the strength to wake up and tell her so she'd know. She *had* to tell her. Angie burst into tears again but she was angry more than anything.

"That bitch Kayla!" She said to herself.

She sat in her car and dialed Kayla's number.

She didn't answer.

Angie knew she probably saw her number and didn't answer because she was still upset at her. She didn't care. She left a voicemail message.

"I know you told Shawn about the whole thing with Deena and Aaron. Now my friend is laid up in the hospital in critical condition!" She cried hard again. "I don't know if he did somethin' to her car or what, but you got what you wanted and now you don't have to worry about speaking to me again EV-ER!"

She hung up the phone and reached in her purse grabbing a handful of Kleenex. She tried to gather herself before driving away.

Her phone rang. It was Kayla calling right back. Angie didn't want to hear her pour salt in the wound and a repeat of her "karma's a bitch" line so she hesitated to answer. It was so like Kayla to do that in this case. She knew she could just hang up if Kayla ever began to utter those words or anything close to it. Her phone was on the third ring.

She answered.

"What?!" She said in a mad voice.

"Before you call accusing me of anything, do your homework first!" Kayla screamed. "I don't know what you're talking about and don't know that man to tell him anything!"

Angie cut her off.

"You're the only one who knew about it, so how else did he find out?!" She screamed back.

"I don't know but it wasn't me. I figured you and your so-called best friend would slip up and bring yourselves down eventually. You didn't need me to do it."

Angie didn't believe her.

"Please. Stop lying. Since you always wanna be tough shit, own up to it."

"I'm not gonna say it again! It wasn't me!" Kayla yelled. "You can't tell me after all this time I'm the only one who knew about it. Go back into that dumb brain of yours and figure out where you slipped up! Get the fuck off my phone!"

Kayla hung up.

Angie threw her phone down on the seat. For a second, she thought about what Kayla said. For a second, she believed her. Deena wasn't able to tell her how Shawn found out and they both knew Kayla was the only person who could tell him. She thought about Toni, but knew if Toni figured it out, she would've gone straight to Deena with it first. She was convinced Kayla did it. She knew if not directly, Kayla at least told someone about it and it got back to Shawn. She knew Kayla better than anyone. She was good at doing something and not having the finger pointed at her.

Angie started up her car and slowly backed out of the parking spot. Her eyes were still red. She drove away from the hospital and said a little prayer for Deena.

CHAPTER 34

Deena's accident had been shown on the evening news. Her car flipped on its side on the grassy hill off the freeway was the image flashed. Angie had made it back to her mother's house by then and saw it. She was devastated all over again. Deena would never drive reckless to the point of flipping her own car over. She replayed what Deena said. She was frustrated that she could only make out certain words. Whatever it was, it had something to do with Shawn knowing about Aaron.

It hit Angie that she hadn't even thought about how Shawn felt. He had to be upset at what they did and rightfully so. If he did do something to cause Deena's accident, was he coming after *her* now? He knew what area she lived in. Deena told him where she was coming from when she dropped Aaron off to him at work that one day. Angie didn't know what connections he had to find out her exact address and she didn't want to take any chances.

She looked at her mother. Shawn didn't know anything about her or where she lived. She could lay low there for at least a week just in case. She couldn't dare tell her what was going on. Her mother would revert back to looking down on her again and she didn't want to ruin their good relationship. Angie needed her more than ever.

Her mother was in the kitchen giving Aaron some Jell-O.

"Mom, you mind if we stay here tonight?" Angie asked.

She told her she was wiped out and stressed over Deena. She needed to lie down and get some rest to clear her head.

"Sure. Go lay down in my bed and get some sleep," her mother said. She pointed to Aaron and smiled. "I'll occupy this one while Tia gets her homework done."

"Okay," Angie said.

She knew Tia had pajamas there. She told her to shower before going to bed and they'd go home in the morning for her to get dressed for school. Her mother told her she'd take Tia home in the morning to get a change of clothes and drive her to school for her. It left Angie relieved. All she had to do was drop Aaron off at daycare and head straight back to the hospital to see Deena.

"I'm gonna ask off work tomorrow to go back to the hospital. They won't give me any information over the phone because I'm just a friend," Angie complained to her mother.

She had to call Deena's grandmother for any updates.

"Well go sit over there most of the day," her

mother told her. "Sometimes when you do that, you can call back to that certain nurse and she'll give you information knowing who you are."

"Yeah I'll do that. I'm sure they won't let me take off work for more days. This is a new job and I can't afford to anyway."

Angie hoped Deena would start to get better soon. She went and laid across her mother's bed and called Deena's grandmother. She told her Deena never woke up during their visit. She was having surgery early the next morning. Angie told her she would go and sit with her most of the day. They hung up and Angie buried her face in the pillow and cried quietly. She wished she knew what really happened.

The next day she made it to the hospital after Deena was out of surgery. She was hoping she'd wake up but she had slipped into a coma during the surgery. Her nurse told Angie they weren't sure when she'd wake up, but it could be at least a few days to a few weeks. She explained to her that in some cases, it took even longer. Angie turned into a crying mess again.

"Are you best friends?" The nurse asked.

Angie could only shake her head yes. She stood by Deena's bed staring at her. The nurse walked over and rubbed her back to console her.

"You can still talk to her or maybe read some of her favorite things," the nurse said softly. "Some people play music too."

"Okay," Angie said sobbing.

"Let me know if you need anything. I'm her nurse until seven o'clock tonight so I'll be here all day," she said.

Angie thanked her and she left the room. She broke again.

She turned away from Deena.

"Oh my God Deena what did we do?" She whispered to herself.

Angie felt like she was just as responsible for Deena's condition, allowing her to fool Shawn with Aaron. At the same time, she cursed Kayla in her own head and still blamed her for telling Shawn. She turned back around to Deena. She looked almost lifeless laying there. Angie rubbed her hair and tried to shape it around her head in place. It had been flattened out across the pillows. She looked around the room at the drabness. She flicked some light switches that brightened the spot over Deena's bed and turned the TV on.

"If you're gonna be here for a while, we gotta make it yours," Angie said to her. "I'll be right back."

She got herself together and wiped her eyes. She left and went to buy balloons at the gift shop. She came back with one oversized GET WELL SOON one and four shiny purple and teal ones. They were Deena's favorite colors. She carried a small potted plant in her other hand. She put the balloons in the corner of the room out of the way of Deena's monitoring machines and placed the plant on the window sill. The nurse had come back and lowered her bed down a little so Angie could sit next to it and talk to her. She did that most of the day. Shawn was not brought up or what she thought of Kayla. She didn't want to damper Deena's spirits or make her feel guilty about anything in her current state, just in case she could actually hear her. It constantly crossed her mind while she sat there. She couldn't help but think if Deena were to die, she'd never really know what happened to her friend and if Shawn was responsible. It tore her up inside. She used those moments to turn her chair around and let out her cries. She was tempted to call Shawn and yell and scream, but she had no proof of anything. Deena had only been able to say something the best way she could in her condition. Angie replayed what she said. It killed her to know. She could only hope the coma would last just a few days and Deena would pull through like the nurse said. There was nothing to do but wait.

⫘⫘⫘«◉»⫘⫘⫘

Angie stayed at her mother's for almost the entire week. Her mother had been helping pick up the kids so she could go see Deena after work. She still had not come out of her coma. Angie had only missed one day of going to see her. She was mentally drained and had passed out asleep in her mother's bed after work. When she woke up, visiting hours were over. She called Deena's nurse that night to check on her and there was no change. Her mother was right that since she had been visiting every day, the nurses would give her information over the phone.

It was Sunday and Angie called the hospital to check on her. There was still no change and the nurse had given her word that if Deena showed any response, she would call her right away. She planned on going that afternoon after she went back home for the first time to do laundry. Her mother and Aaron had formed a bond. He always woke up right after she did and sat with her in the kitchen while she made her morning coffee. Angie looked over at him from the living room. He rolled his toy cars back and forth while he and her mother talked. She seemed to understand most of his toddler talk or at least she just agreed with him when she didn't.

Angie's phone rang and she grabbed for it quickly thinking it was the hospital. She didn't recognize the number but she answered just in case.

"Hello," she said.

It was a female voice she didn't know.

"At least your mother had the decency to tell Shawn the truth. This is not over."

She hung up. Angie almost dropped the phone.

It was Shawn's wife.

Angie's mother was at the bank across the street from Shawn's transport business when Deena got there to pick up Aaron the prior week. She saw Shawn bringing Aaron out to Deena. She didn't know Shawn but was curious as to why her grandson was with a strange man being handed off to Deena. With what Tia told her about thinking Deena wanted to be Aaron's mom, she made her way over to the transport business to find out what was going on. Shawn was still at the front door.

"Excuse me. My name is Sherry," she said.

Shawn shook her hand and asked how he could help.

"I noticed the little boy you brought out to the woman who just left with him."

"Yeah, that's my son," Shawn said with a frown, curious about what she was getting at.

"Okay, well he's *my* grandson," she said.

"Grandson?" Shawn asked. "His mother told me both her parents died years ago."

"Why would Angie tell you that?"

"Angie?! No, I'm talking about Deena."

Shawn looked more confused. Angie's mother wrinkled her eyebrows and stared at him. She reached in her purse and took out her wallet.

"I have a picture of him. See."

She showed Shawn a picture of Aaron that Angie had given her.

"Yeah that's Xavier," Shawn said.

"No. His name is Aaron," she said. "And here's a picture of him, Angie, and my granddaughter Tia."

She showed him another picture of the three of them.

"I'm Angie's mother and she's Aaron's mother. Not Deena."

Shawn stared closely at the pictures and then stared back at her.

"That BITCH!" He yelled.

Angie's mother was shocked at his response and tried to explain that she didn't mean to meddle. She told him she only wanted to know why Deena was picking her grandson up from him. He didn't say anything else to her and ran into the back office out of the lobby. Seeing how upset he was, she turned and left quickly. She never told Angie anything about it.

Angie still didn't know exactly how her mother had even come into contact with Shawn and what all she told him. Shawn's wife hadn't said all that. Her hands shook and she could barely sit her phone down. She looked over at her mother in the kitchen. Did she know Shawn caused Deena's accident? She had never asked to go along to visit her at the hospital. Angie stood up from the couch and stared at her in a rage.

She forced one foot in front of the other and walked into the kitchen toward her. Her mind raced as she stared at her, taking each step.

"What did you do?!" she yelled out. "How did you even know?!"

Angie's eyes widened and for a time she hadn't even blinked. Her mother looked up from putting a dish into the sink. She stepped backward seeing Angie coming at her.

"Know what?!" She was surprised and confused.

She bumped into the rack in her kitchen backing up. Angie stopped.

"About Aaron! You told him about Aaron," Angie said. She looked over at him. His little eyes were looking back at her hearing his name.

Her mother knew right away what she meant. She had never told Angie about it because she had obviously exposed a secret between her and Deena. She spoke fast to explain, focusing on the rage in Angie's eyes.

"Angie, I didn't know about anything. I swear," she said.

She told Angie about how she saw Shawn handing Aaron to Deena in the parking lot at the transport company and that she simply went to him and told him she was Aaron's grandmother. She explained how their conversation went and how Shawn suddenly reacted.

"I wasn't trying to get in your business and I realized at that moment what I did," she said. "I just didn't know how to tell you and I should've let you know what happened."

Angie turned to walk away and put her hands on her head.

"Oh my God. I can't believe this."

She paced back and forth across the living room. Her mother stood still watching her. She knew it was the phone call Angie had gotten.

"What happened? Who was that on the phone?" She asked.

"I don't know. But the person said at least *you* had the decency to tell Shawn and this isn't over,"

Angie said. "I think he did something to make Deena crash her car, but I'm not sure."

She sat down on the couch and stared at the floor. Her mind went back to the phone call.

"Call the police," her mother said. "If you think he's responsible they can at least try to find out where he was that morning and go from there."

Angie didn't say anything. She didn't want to call the police or anyone because she'd have to explain the mess they created. That, to her was just as bad. Her phone rang again and she jumped slightly. She grabbed it quick and looked.

It was Deena's grandmother. The hospital had called and told her Deena was out of her coma. Angie thanked her and hung up the phone.

"She came out of the coma," Angie said to her mother.

She ran to put her shoes on to rush to the hospital.

"That's a relief. Go!" Her mother said. "I'll pick up Tia from school."

Angie drove to the hospital. She wasn't sure how to tell Deena it was her mother who told Shawn about Aaron. She parked and walked as fast as she could to get to her room. She almost brisk walked past the family waiting area when she saw Deena's grandmother and uncle. They had been asked to wait in there instead of Deena's room for the doctor to speak with them about her condition. Angie waited with them.

"You got here fast," her grandmother said.

"I left as soon as you called me," she said.

She had sat down to catch her breath. She looked at Deena's grandmother. She was small and frail, holding her cane next to her in the chair. Deena's uncle walked back and forth, at times looking up at the television mounted on the wall.

"What's taking them so long?" he said.

His impatience got the better of him. He stepped in the hallway to see if the doctor was coming.

Three of them were headed toward the waiting room all with their long white doctor coats and stethoscopes around their necks. They came in and Angie stared at them, waiting for whatever it was that had to be said out of Deena's ear shot.

It was bad news. Deena was paralyzed from the waist down.

"Ohh dear God!" her grandmother cried out.

She let go of her cane and it fell to the floor. She was helplessly looking up at the doctors from her chair. Angie pressed her hands against her mouth to keep her own gasps quiet. She was in disbelief.

They explained her diagnosis mostly in medical terms only they understood. Angie tuned them out with the image of Deena in a wheelchair. The doctors hadn't told her yet and said they'd come back in a short while to discuss things with her. She was still not fully alert from the effects of the pain meds.

"Take me to the chapel in here Patrick," Deena's grandmother said. "I need to go and say a prayer for her."

Her uncle went over to her and helped her to her feet. She told Angie to go in and sit with Deena until they came back. Angie walked down the hall to the room. She teared up still picturing Deena that way. She reached the room and took a deep breath before stepping in. She forced a smile and walked to the bed. Deena was asleep, but opened her eyes as Angie got closer.

"Hey friend," she said.

"Hey," Deena said in a groggy, half-awake voice.

Angie rubbed her hair backward to smooth it out. She wasn't sure if Deena even knew she had been in coma. She wasn't going to bring it up.

"Your grandmother and uncle are here," Angie said. "They'll be right back."

"Okay."

Deena looked around the room. She moved one of her hands from under the covers and scanned herself. She focused on her feet, noticing them in blue hospital booties.

"I can't feel my legs," she said.

Angie softened her eyes and looked at her.

"I know."

CPSIA information can be obtained
at www.ICGtesting.com
Printed in the USA
JSHW020015050522
25541JS00005B/22

9 781977 244659